The Tale of the Murderous

Southern Belle

I0417800

By

J.F. Fleming

If I had never picked up an Elmore Leonard novel,

I might have never tried to write a fiction of crime.

Chapter I

The First Encounter with Ellanece Mosley

In the small town of Bucksdale, Mississippi, Detective Jasper Lewis, arrived at the scene of a home invasion, where he pulled up to an old run-down Victorian, which sat at 300 East Church Street. As he stepped out into the humid summer night's air, he observed how the home was riddled with cracked windows, peeling paint, loose floor boards, and missing more than a few shingles. It was the type of place that all the neighbor kids, rumored to be haunted. The home was owned by a new comer to the town, twenty-eight-year-old, Ellanece Mosley, a beautiful young southern belle, who found herself the unfortunate victim of what appeared to be a home invasion/attempted rape.

As the Detective approached her, he was taken by her long, wavy, black hair, blue eyes, and soft pink lips. She sat on the front porch of her home, wrapped in a white afghan blanket. Just before hitting the steps, he stopped, made eye contact with her, and said, "Ms. Mosley, I'm Detective Lewis, with the BPD. I'll be heading up this investigation. I hate we had to meet under these circumstances, just sit tight, while I go examine the body and I'll be back in a few moments to ask you a few questions." Ellanece remained silent, but nodded, to show that she understood. He then continued to make his way into the house.

The entire time he was walking through the home, he was shocked that a woman as beautiful as Ellanece, lived in such a dilapidated place. He made his way into the foyer, through the living room, and into the kitchen where the dead corpse lay. There on the old rotted hardwood floor was the body of one, Dennis Henderson, a thirty-two-year-old male, with no prior arrest record.

The man had suffered from several lacerations to the upper body and head. The murder weapon, a large meat cleaver, with a stainless steel blade, and smooth polished red oak handle, still stuck in the man's skull. Lewis looked around the kitchen for a moment, every now and then glancing back at the late Mr. Henderson. He then looked to one of the other uniformed Officers, and asked, "Where exactly did the *perp* break in?"

"There was no point of, forced entry," the Officer responded, "all evidence points out that if anything—he was let into the home."

"I thought that this was a home invasion case?"

"It is! Or at least, that's what the lady called it in as."

Lewis stood there for a few more moments, all the while logging notes into his iPhone. When he was done with the note taking, he began to snap pictures with the phone's camera. He photographed the kitchen as a whole, he got a close up of the corpse, and an even closer shot of the cranium-stuck cleaver. After he was finished, he placed the phone into his left back pocket, and made his way out of the house, back to where Ellanece sat awaiting his return. "Ms. Mosley, at this time, I'm afraid I'm going to have to place you under arrest, for the murder of Denis Henderson. Once I got you down at the station, I'm gonna have to book you, and ask you a few questions."

Ellanece was quick to her feet and with a distressed fearful look on her face, she inquired, "I'm being arrested? He's the one who broke into my house!" to which the Detective promptly responded, "Yes, ma'am I understand that, but never the less you've still killed a man. Understand you're only being charged with murder; you haven't been convicted of anything yet. I'm sure once this goes to trial, evidence will prove you were in the right and the whole thing will be dropped.

"But until that time, I still have to bring you in for questioning. Trust me, as soon is the questioning is done, you'll be free to make bail." Biting her knuckles, hesitant to comply, she looked up to Detective Lewis, "What's my bail set at?" Getting his cuffs ready, he replied, "Twenty-thousand dollars." Taking a few steps back she exclaimed, *"Twenty-thousand dollars*! I don't have that kind of cash."

Lewis slowly nodded his head, "Yes ma'am that's why you'll need to call you a bondsman, we have all the numbers listed down at the station, you'll call the bondsman of your preference, and once they post bail for you, you'll pay them ten percent of the bail, which is only two-thousand dollars…And most bondsmen have finance plans available if you don't have the full payment readily available." Nodding her head and taking in a deep breath she replied, "Aight, let's go on and get this over with."

Lewis paused for a moment and then inquisitively added, "Ma'am, just so you know; only *guilty people* are afraid to get booked and questioned." Not wanting to seem any more suspicious than she knew she probably already looked, she was very quick to nod her head, holding out her hands to be cuffed. Lewis, placed the cuffs on her as gently as possible, read her the Miranda rights and continued to escort her down to his blacked out police cruiser.

After placing her into the vehicle he made his way over to the driver side seat of the cruiser. He cranked the car and drove away from the scene. As they drove towards the station, Ellanece's beauty seemed to increase to the Detective. Knowing that this was dangerous, and that as an Officer of the Law, it was his duty to not let a charming young woman, beguile him, in any way. He decided to occupy the silence with some preliminary questioning.

"You ain't from around here, are ya?" he asked. Ellanece took her time to answer. Contemplating on how much personal information she should let the detective in on. "No. I'm from Alabama." he turned his nose up at her, and scoffed in a joking manner; to try and lighten the mood, and said, "Oh no! So I take it you're not an Ole Miss fan, are ya?" letting out a light sigh she answered, "No I'm not. Nor am I a State fan."

"So, what part of the great sister state of Mississippi do you hail from?"

"Alec City," she replied. Lewis scratched his head, commenting, "Don't think I've ever heard of that one, which county is it in?"

"I'm sorry, *Alec* or *Alex* City, is what us locals call it. The official name is Alexander City, and it's located in Tallapoosa County." All Lewis could really do was shake his head, "Sorry...I still don't really know where that is, only places I go in Alabama are: Tuscaloosa for football, and Gulf Shores for the beach."

It wasn't long before they pulled up outside of the police station, and Detective Lewis escorted Ellanece in for booking and questioning. Upon entering the station, which to Ellanece had an overbearingly strong bleach odor to it; a uniformed officer met them and escorted Ellanece over to booking, where she was finger printed, and had her mugshot taken. It wasn't long before she was reunited with Lewis, and they entered an interrogation room.

Lewis calmly shut the door behind them, and took a seat across the table from her. They sat in silence for a moment, almost as if they were in some sort of staring contest. Breaking the silence, Lewis leaned back in his chair and said, "Okay...I'll start. Ms. Mosley, do you know the name of the, 'alleged' home intruder; the one that lies *dead* on your kitchen floor?" Ellanece leaned forward clasping her hands together, and resting her elbows onto the table. "Yea, his name's Dennis—or at least that's what he told me it was."

"Right, and did Dennis ever tell you his last name?"

"Yea, it was something like Anderson or Henderson, wasn't it?"

"Yes, Dennis Henderson, is the name of the man that lies *dead* in the middle of your kitchen floor, with a meat cleaver lodged firmly in his skull. Would you care to elaborate on how that cleaver came to rest there?" Ellanece carelessly shrugged her shoulders, and without any hesitation she said, "Yea, I put it there!"

Shaking his head in disappointment, Lewis replied, "I'm aware of who put it there! What I would like to know, is what the hell Mr. Henderson was even doing at your home in the first place? What provoked him to attack you? And last but not least…why is there no point of forced entry, when you clearly called it in as a home invasion?" Ellanece took her time to answer; trying to think of how she was going to word her story, "Sure—"

"—Might I also add," the Detective interrupted, "before you decide to give me your, *official statement* that Mr. Henderson has never once been arrested." Ellanece cleared her throat and continued, "—As I was saying, Detective, I moved here to the town of Bucksdale a little over six months ago. I bought the old Victorian house with plans of restoring it, and selling it for twice, maybe even triple the price of what I bought it for.

"That's how I make my living; I flip houses. Anyway, I've been stuck in this town for months, and everything imaginable that could go wrong—has! So earlier today, I went out and bought me two bottles of white zinfandel, and had me a few glasses." Trying to hurry Ellanece up; Lewis interrupted her once more, "Ma'am, I'm sorry I hate to interrupt ya, but can you move on to the point, it's almost midnight, and I would like to get home at some point in time tonight. So, cut the life story, and tell me why and how Mr. Henderson has a giant-ass knife hanging out of his head?"

Ellanece sat in her chair cutting her eyes very intensely, at the detective. "Look son, you're the one that's brought me down here, booking me and all, blacking up my fingers and such, I'll tell you my story the way I think it needs to be told. I don't take very kindly to being hassled! After all— that's how Mr. Henderson wound up dead in the first place."

Now confused more than ever, Lewis came to his feet and leaned across the table, and said in a very stern voice, "Ms. Mosley, you mean to tell me that you murdered a man, all because he *rushed* you? I'm sorry Ms. Mosley, but I don't think that being rushed by someone, is a valid reason for murder!" Hopping out of her chair, to meet the Detective's intense stare at the middle of the table, she shouted out, "It is when *sex* is involved!"

Startled at what he had just heard, Lewis took a few steps back, and in astonishment said, "What?" thumping back into her chair with a caustic attitude, she continued, "That's right Detective, you heard me! Now, do you wanna hear the rest of my story? Or do you just wanna go ahead lock me up for killing a guy who tried to rush me into sex?" Trying his best not to lose his composure, he sat back down and scooted his chair up to the table. He folded his hands down on top of each other, and stated, "No ma'am, please…continue."

Knowing that she now had the reigns of the interrogation in her hands, she flipped her hair out of her face, and said, "Okay, so I've got a couple of glasses of wine in me, it's getting late, I ain't got no TV or WiFi, so I'm streaming on my 4G phone, using God only knows how much data, and I find myself looking through the *personals* section on my Craig's list app. Now, as much as I hate to admit it, I was feeling kinda lonely, and not that it's any of your business, but it's been over three years since I been physical with a man, and even longer than that since I've been in a serious relationship with one.

"So, I'm tipsy, I'm horny, and I put out an ad on Craig's list stating: that I'm *horny* and in the mood. Well as I am sure you can imagine, just about every guy within fifteen miles answered my post. I picked Mr. Henderson at random, and we exchanged e-mails. We chatted for an hour or so, during which time I sent him a few pictures of my boobs, and he sent me a few of his junk. All the while, I have two more glasses of wine. Well, after chatting and exchanging *naughty* pictures, I say to myself: *To hell with it Ella, you work hard! Let off a little steam, and ride some stranger, letting him give ya everything he's got!* So, I foolishly gave him directions to my house.

The dude takes forever to make his way over to my place. Which by the time he shows up, and calls me to say he is outside, I'm more than half-drunk, not to mention I'm tired, and ready for bed! I didn't want to be rude. Also, I was feeling a little guilty for leading him on. So I went to the door and flagged him in.

"When he got inside, he didn't waste any time trying to shove his nasty tongue down my throat. I pushed him away, and explained my situation. So, after all my explaining, I tell him that maybe if he will be cool about me flaking out on him; that maybe we could get together another time. Ya know, after we get to know each other just a little better. But Mr. Henderson isn't having any part of it. He immediately becomes heated, slamming his palms against the walls of my living room, every time that he tries to make some outlandish point.

"Well, as he is slamming his palms into my already dilapidated walls. The business woman in me kicks in, and gets onto him for potentially damaging my property. So I demand that he leave. That's when he charged me, pushed me up against a wall, and slid his dirty hands from my hips up to my torso, and as he squeezes my boobs, he says to me, 'Bitches ain't shit but ho's and tricks, and I'm not going to leave, empty handed!'

"So thinking as quickly as I could, I tell him that if he will just let me go to my kitchen to pour some more booze down my throat; that I will get so hammered, that I'll damn near let him do anything he wants to me. Surprise, surprise, the bastard does what I ask, he lets go, and takes himself a seat on a stepping stool, and tells me that he will be sitting there waiting. So I make my way into the kitchen, where the first thing I do is grab the biggest sharpest knife that I can find.

"I then whip my phone out, and dial 911 for help. I didn't know what else to classify it as, but a *home invasion*, and I tell them that they really need to hurry! By the time I turn around, he is standing in the kitchen threshold, and asks what the hell it was that I thought I was doing. It was right then and there that I decided that I was going to fight and not let myself become a victim! So I charged him! I slashed him a couple of time around the chest, and ribs. I half hoped that he would make a run for it, out of fear for his life, but he just kept shuffling around in circles, swatting and throwing stuff at me."

That's when Ellanece paused, and pointed to the back of her head, right behind her ear, and revealed a large bump. "Bastard managed to get me a few times, as you can see! Anyway, my gut just kicked in, and I thought to myself: *Nail this guy! Before it's too late, and he gains the upper hand!* So when a window opened up, I jumped on him, wrapping my legs around his waist, and I slung that cleaver down as hard as I could...I never in my wildest dreams thought a knife could slice through a man's head like butter. Then before I know it, he's lying dead on my floor, and y'all showed up, not ten minutes later."

Lewis was now pacing back and forth, with his hand fixed to his chin. "That's a very compelling story, Ms. Mosley. You wouldn't happen to know, how old Mr. Henderson was, would you?" Shaking her head and shrugging her shoulders, she replied, "Naw, not really, I mean, if I had to guess, I would say late twenties, early thirties?"

Detective Lewis nodded his head and shook his finger at her, confirming she was close, "The deceased was thirty-two! Now you know what I find to be so troubling about that?" Ellanece shrugged, and replied, "Hell I don't know, maybe that you didn't catch this sex offender sooner?" Lewis threw his hand out, pointing to her, and exclaimed, "Exactly!" he then continued pacing, and carried on with his explanation, "Men who display any form of sexual perversion often times, show it first, in their adolescent years.

"Often times getting caught and arrested between the ages of fourteen and twenty; may I emphasize, once again, on how clean, Mr. Henderson's record was. I'm even sure that if I do a little digging I'll find that he was probably somewhat of a model student, back in high school. He was born and raised here in Bucksdale, after all. I even think I remember sharing a gym class or two with him. Not that we were pals or ever talked, I'm a couple of years older than him."

"Are you saying that you don't believe what I have just told you?" shaking his head the Detective politely corrected her, "No ma'am, not at all! I'm simply stating that I am going to double, maybe even triple check every detail there is!" Now sitting with her arms crossed, aggravated, that the Detective wasn't completely buying her story as easily as she had hoped he would, she asked, "Are you done with your questions? And if you are, may I go?"

The Detective, took a few steps back over to the table, and as he leaned against it, cocked his head to the side in a very debonair fashion and said, "Naw—that's it! You're free to go." Ellanece didn't waste any time getting out of her chair, heading for the door, but before she could even get half way across the room, Lewis delivered his final statement, "Oh and Ms. Mosley, as they say in the movies, *don't leave town.* Because, this investigation is far from over; I might even suggest you getting a lawyer, in the near future."

Ellanece stopped to turn around and said, "I had every right to kill that man! He was gonna rape me if I didn't! I'm innocent; dammit!" to which the Detective fired back, "Everyone is, until proven guilty, in a court of law!" Ellanece just sneered, and continued to wait till a Uniformed Officer escorted her to a payphone, so that she could call a bondsman.

Chapter II

The Murder of Dennis Henderson

Two weeks prior to the alleged home invasion. Ellanece pulled up outside of the Bucksdale Baptist Church, in her 1999 forest green Pontiac Firebird. She stepped out of her vehicle wearing pink Sketchers, a black pair of sweatpants, with the words *juicy* written on the seat, and a baggy t-shirt, without the slightest amount of make up on.

   She entered the doors of the humble little church, and as she made her way through the halls, she entered into a room with a sign that read: *Sex Addicts Anonymous Community Group Meeting.* Upon entering the room, she stopped at a table to pour her some coffee and grabbed a few doughnuts. She then continued to make her way back over to the center of the room, where a circle of fold out chairs had been arranged. She took her seat, and waited for the meeting to begin. Here in this room, she would choose her unsuspecting victim.

   The seats around her quickly filled, and it wasn't long before the doors to the room were closed, and a man wearing loafers, blue jeans, a button up shirt accented by a sports blazer, took a seat amongst the collected circle of people. The man was an elderly gentleman with subtle wrinkles lining his face, he was bald up top, but in the back he had silvery silk hair, that was pulled back into a pony tail that stopped at his shoulder blades. As the room settled down, he cleared his throat, so he could speak, "Hi, as most of you already know, my name is Dr. John Carroll, and I am the head counselor of Sex Addicts Anonymous. I see a few new faces in the crowd; for those of you who are new, or simply just may not be aware of how SAA works, you are not required to speak.

   "However, feel free to raise your hand and say what's on your mind, whenever you feel comfortable enough to do so. SAA is a group that much like other similar groups such as AA and NA is based around a simple twelve step, self-help program, where addicts help other addicts. As I look out amongst the group; I can see that we have four of our regular sponsors here with us tonight. So, to any of you, new people, who feel like you would like to get a sponsor, feel free to seek any one of them out at the end of the meeting; and just so we all know who you are, would my four regulars please stand and introduce yourselves."

The first person to stand up was a young lady who appeared to be in her early twenties, she had shoulder length brown hair with red highlights, a piercing over her left eyebrow. Both her ear lobes were gauged out to a fairly noticeable size. She wore a punk rock attire, and as she took a moment, before speaking, she looked around the room, almost as if she was checking to make sure that there wasn't someone in the crowd, who she didn't want to hear what she had to say, after the pause, she began to speak, "Sup guys? My name is Amanda; I'm twenty-three years old. I've been clean and sober for the past two years. I'm now in a steady committed relationship with one of the most wonderful guys *God* could have ever placed on this earth.

"I can also safely say that three years ago from today, I never thought that I would be so *blessed* with what's been given to me, in my life. Feel free to come and ask me about any questions that you may have after the meeting, I promise that no matter what you're going through, I've been through similar, or worse, and that no matter how

terribly gruesome you think your life might be right
now, that I am what they call a *judgment-free-zone*,
so please, feel free to tell me whatever you need to
get off of your chest. Well, that about sums it up
from me; and I hope everyone has a blessed and
wonderful day."

The young lady sat down, and a middle aged
man, three chairs across from her stood up. The
man looked rough, like he had seen some hard
situations in his day. He had a gray handlebar
mustache with spiked salt and peppered hair, he
wore just a regular white T-shirt, with a blue
unbuttoned work shirt over it, that held a pack of
Marlboro Red cigarettes, in the chest pocket, "Hi
y'all, I'm Gus. I'm forty-five years old, and I'm
here to tell you that there ain't a thang in this world,
that you can tell me 'bout, that will shock me, or
make me think any less of you.

"I've done it all, man! The whole shebang!
Everything from: alcohol, to sex, drugs, and rock &
roll. I've lost a lot of friends over the past forty-five
years to this addiction, and I by my own actions,
have contracted two STDs, Herpes and HIV. Again,
I'm Gus, and I'm here if ya need me."

The next person that followed was a man in
his early thirties; he had short red curly matted hair,
about two day's growth of facial hair. Thick black
framed glasses, and dressed like a typical hipster;
everything from his obnoxiously tight jeans, to the
gamer T-shirt he wore, that screamed, *look at how
nerdishly smart I am.*

He even shyly waved to the group, before he
spoke, as if he felt it was necessary in order to

commence speaking, "Hey guy's, what's happening? My name is Dennis, and I'm a sex addict. I've been in the SAA program since I was twenty-three. However, I've only been attending meetings at this particular group, for the past two years. My whole thing used to be soliciting sex via the internet. Chat rooms, sex forums, dating sights, hook-up-sights, you name it.

"As most of you probably know, in order to sponsor, you have to be clean and sober for at least one year; and I am here to tell you, that I have gotten myself clean many times; I have also *relapsed* many times. A few of those times costing me my position to sponsor to fellow addicts. I've now been clean for the past year and a half and have recently been re-granted a sponsorship roll. So if you feel like you might be at risk for relapsing, hit me up. Because, I have totally been there, and can undoubtedly confirm that it is so not worth it."

The last person to get up and stand was a woman whom looked to be in her early sixties. She looked like the type of person, that if you hadn't seen her at the meeting, you never would have guessed that she would have ever had the need to show up for one, "Hi gang, my name is Monica, much like the rest of you, I have been addicted to the *feeling* that sex gives me, for the majority of my life. I lost my virginity when I was sixteen years old, I lost it to my high school sweetie, whom I would later go on to marry after we graduated! Yes, the same high school sweetheart that would later, continue to have multiple affairs on me, behind my back.

"Well, after I came wise to it, I did the *Christian* thing, and forgave him, and even helped put him in an organization very similar to this one. I wanted the love of my life, to get the best help he could find. Because, even way back then I could recognize, that this was a disease! It wasn't his choice to get stuck with it. It just sort of happened, right? Wrong!

"I firmly believe that deep down sexual-deviancy is something that you choose. After we got him help, he continued to cheat on me, and after realizing he was beyond guidance of the church; I divorced him in 1982. After the divorce, I decided that I was going to go to some bars, (much like my former husband) and get all of the *ass* that I could. It wasn't until I contracted an STD that I made the choice to put myself in SAA; and try to live the best life for not only me, but also, for my children as well."

As Monica sat down, everyone in the circle clapped, including Dr. Carroll. After everyone settled down, the people started to make their rounds, sharing their stories and experiences. The entire time Ellanece sat twiddling her thumbs, nervous about whether she was going to stand up and speak or not. The meeting was only an hour long, and it was no time before it was closing to an end. Dr. Carroll spoke out and gave a last call for anyone who wanted to speak. Ellanece knew that it was now or never, so she raised her hand, and waited to be called on. After waiting patiently, it was finally her time to speak to the group.

Ellanece stood up and began to say her piece. "Hi y'all, my name is—*Stella*, and I like others of you have mentioned, solicit sex over the internet. I've done it sober before, but I mainly only do it after I have gotten a few drinks into me. The more intoxicated I get, the worse my situation winds up. From having sex with multiple partners at once to even banging it out with members of the same sex.

"One night I got black out drunk, and somewhere along the way snapped out of my blacked out state of mind, and realized that I was having sex with not just one but two different partners. It was really scary for me! I remembered going online, but I had absolutely no memory of chatting with anyone; let alone inviting two *strangers* into my home to have sex with me.

"Anyway, that's my story for tonight, I've been clean for… maybe a week? *Dennis* wasn't joking when he said the relapse thing, is more than easy to happen to someone, than you might think. I mean, it's a terrible thing when you wake up one day and realize that you are completely addicted to something that not only now disgusts you! But also, mortally frightens you. This world is a pretty messed-up place when you really start to look at all the nasty details. Well that's just about all I gotta say, thanks for listening." Ellanece waved to the group to signal that she was done, and continued to take a seat.

It wasn't long before Dr. Carroll brought the meeting to a close. After the meeting had been adjourned, is when Ellanece decided that she was going to make her move. She made her way through the crowd of people, over to the refreshments table, where she saw Dennis talking to some of the other members of the group. She waited patiently for her turn, and after he was done talking, she tapped him on the shoulder and stuck her hand out for him to shake.

"Hi I'm Stella! It was so good to hear that there was somebody else *just like me* out there. I mean, I expected to be around other sex addicts, duh. But I never thought there would be someone who went about getting it, the same way that I did." Dennis took in a deep breath, before he started talking. "Yea, believe it or not, our method of soliciting and obtaining sex, it's actually pretty popular amongst people our age. It's even starting to gain popularity with some of the older crowds too."

Ellanece made it a point to keep eye contact, to let Dennis know that she was interested, the entire time that he was talking. When he was through, she winced at him, and asked, "I don't know if this is too soon or not, I'm not really familiar with the procedure, but I was wondering if you would sponsor me?" A smile dawned across Dennis's face, and he replied with, "Ya know, as much as I would love to sponsor you Stella, I just can't do it—let me tell you why. You are very cute, we are both around the same age, and we both have high tendencies for relapsing. I'm afraid that if I sponsored you, it would only do more harm, than good.

"Also, it's only in special cases that people can sponsor the opposite sex. Or at least that's the rules in this group. I think that the best person for you would be Monica, she is older and very wise, I think she has a lot of information that she can pass down to you. Anyways, I gotta hit the road, or I'm going to be late for work…It was nice to meet you, good luck with your addiction!" Disappointed that she was not able to land Dennis as her sponsor, and that she had probably just missed a golden opportunity to find herself another victim, she decided that it was probably best if she just headed home.

Back in her *real life* as, Ellanece Mosley, she really did flip houses for a living, and had indeed purchased the run-down Victorian; to flip it for a profit. She had purchased the house as-is, and had spent the first couple of months just getting rid of all the junk that had been left inside from the previous owners, by hosting yard sales, posting things on eBay, and making rounds to local antique shops. Two weeks had passed since her first run in with Dennis, and she had yet to return to the SAA meetings. Mainly because she wasn't addicted to having sex—instead, she was addicted to killing people. In the past week she had experienced nothing but a daunting list of fails.

After appraising the lot and home, her insurance agent gave her a list of all that would need to be fixed in order for an owner to file it on their home owner's insurance, a list that was going to put Ellanece easily fifteen grand in the whole. Not to mention, she still had at least another fifteen thousand, just in cosmetic restorations, and another couple of thousand, in miscellaneous costs. On the day that she murdered Dennis Henderson, she originally had no intentions of meeting with him…let alone killing him.

It was around four-thirty in the afternoon, when Ellanece pulled up to the local neighborhood *Piggly Wiggly* and picked her out two bottles of her favorite brand of White Zinfandel. After purchasing the bottles, she made her way back to her job; which also happened to be her home. She sat in her living room in a fold out lawn chair, sipping on a glass of wine, flipping through her Facebook on her iPhone; as she mind-numbingly scrolled though her feed, her thoughts began to wonder, and as the alcohol set in, doing its job. She got the idea to open up her Craigslist app, and put up a fake post, just to see who all would bite. The post read:

SWFM looking for a good time,

*Hey guys, Tina here. I'm a SWFM about 5'2" 110llbs. I got big tits and a nice ass. Be DDF and send me face pics in your e-mail, and in the subject line write, "Just for Tina" so that I know you are real. Bye for now, I look forward to playing with some stranger tonight, maybe it could be you? *Tina*

After posting the ad, it wasn't long before, just like she had told Detective Lewis, her e-mail account blew up. She maintained a sober enough head, to not respond to any of them, she merely used them as her entertainment for the night. Most of the e-mails were from horny teenagers trying to get lucky. All of the rest were from perverts who sent pictures of their junk, when all she had requested to see, was their face. However, upon all of the single men who posted, she just happened to stumble upon, an e-mail sent from Dennis.

Only, he wasn't going by the name Dennis. Instead, he was using the alias, Jerry Lagrone. He did however; manage to send his real face picture, which is how she was able to determine that it was him. It was almost as if destiny was telling her that she needed to kill this guy, he literally had just fallen into her lap. He sent her a reply that read:

Re: SWFM looking for a good time,
"Just for Tina"

Hey, my name is Jerry Lagrone. I don't do this often, but am in some serious need of a gut locker, to burry myself in. I'm 6'0" 160lbs SWM DDF I'm sending a pic, just like you requested. I hope that you don't leave me hanging.
P.S. Mind sending me a pic of yourself to me?
*Jerry

Ellanece went onto Google, so she could save a fake picture of herself, to her phone, and sent it to Dennis in a message that read:

RE RE: SWFM Looking for a Good Time
'You're Cute'

Hey, here is the pic you asked for. Let me know if ya wanna work something out, I'm SUPER discreet, and am more than willing to host. Below is my number text don't call, and I can give you directions to my house.
*Tina

Dennis of course, unknowingly took the bait, and over a series of texts, that would only lean in Ellanece's favor in the long run; Ellanece guided Dennis, via text message, right to her front door.

As Dennis made his way to the front steps of the rough looking old home, he was a bit concerned. But it helped that the woman, he suspected to be Tina, had warned him about the condition of the house, and also told him, that she was in the middle of renovating it. He knocked three times on the old dirty white door, which gave a rotted thud sound every time his fist made contact.

From the other side of the door, he heard a petite little voice ring out, "Its open, just come on in." Dennis entered into the foyer, and after he didn't see anyone right away, he called out, "Hello," Ellanece replied, "I'm in the kitchen; go ahead and make yourself comfortable there in the living room."

He made his way into the living area, he was once again in shock, over the condition of the place. As Ellanece stood in the kitchen pouring them both a glass of wine, she called out, "Sorry about all the mess, you'll have to bear with me! At the moment my work area, is also my living space. I know it's not the prettiest thing to look at, but I think you will find the bed upstairs, a little more appealing to the eyes."

Dennis took a seat in one of two empty lawn chairs that Ellanece had left out for them. He hadn't been seated long before he jetted up out of the chair when he was surprised to see the woman he thought was *Tina*, was actually the woman he knew as

Stella, standing in the doorway of the living room, holding two glasses of wine.

"Stella, what the hell is going on here?" Ellanece quickly pranced her way over to Dennis, holding out a wine glass for him to take, "Shh," she whispered out, "I swear to God, I didn't intentionally seek you out. You actually sought me out by answering to my Craigslist post and alias that I used. When I saw your picture come up, I thought that it was a sign that you and I were meant to hook-up with one another via our disease of sexual addiction."

As she was now right in front of him, she seductively swirled the wine glass under his nose. "Look babe, I promise that I am super discrete, and if you'll just bang my brains out tonight, you'll never have to worry about hearing from me again." Falling for the act, like she knew he would, he accepted the wine glass, and took a few sips from it. "There now, that wasn't so bad. Was it?" she asked.

Dennis slowly shook his head no. "Please Dennis, have a seat, your making me feel like I'm a bad hostess or something. Dennis hesitantly did as he was told, Ellanece straddling him the moment that he was firmly seated. Once planted, she began to grind in his lap, every now and then pushing her breasts directly into his face.

She could tell by a shifting in his pants that he was becoming aroused, and that Dennis was now hers for the killing. Before he was able to obtain a full erection, she popped off of his lap and asked, "Hey, ya mind if I give ya a tour of the place? I'll take ya all over, and tell you my plans for each room! We'll end the tour in the kitchen, where we can refill our wine glasses, and make our way back up to the bedroom for some *adult play time*.

Helpless to say no, all Dennis was able to do, was to agree to follow Ellanece around the house. They started on the main floor, made their way down to the basement; where she gave a ten-minute bullshit back story, on how back in the civil war, it was used to hide Confederate Soldiers from Yankee Troops.

They finally made their way up stairs, past the main floor, up to the second, where she showed him the bedroom, and whispered into his ear a seductive preview of everything she wanted him to do to her. After she was through showing him the second floor, she asked if he was ready for that refill of wine; to which he was more than happy to say yes to.

They made their way down to the kitchen, where Ellanece took his glass from him and started to fill it up. She paused, and continued to set the wine bottle down. She walked over to where he stood, and seductively twirled her finger on his chest, "Hey, what do ya say, 'to hell with the bedroom for right now?' and we just screw here in the kitchen, with the intent on getting as drunk as we can?"

Dennis placed his hands on her ass and squeezed, and said, "Sounds like a plan to me!" He turned loose of her butt, and began to fidget with his belt buckle. To which Ellanece was very quick to stop, "Whoa babe, not so fast! Let me run upstairs really quick and grab a couple of toys for us to play

with, you need me to bring down a condom?"
Dennis just smiled and said, "Nah I got my own
supply—you really are a kinky bitch, aren't you?"
Ellanece responded by winking, and then made her
way up the stairs.

Once she got to the second floor, she made a
bee line for her bedroom, where she locked herself
in her closet. Once safely locked in, she pulled out
her iPhone, and dialed 911. "Hello, I would like to
report a forced entry; please hurry, I can't tell, but I
think the man has been drinking, he's acting very
belligerent." Ellanece quickly hung up the phone;
she knew that she had no longer than just a few
minutes to kill Dennis. She busted out of her closet,
and rushed down the staircase, back into the kitchen
where she met back up with Dennis.

"I thought you said you were running up, to
grab some toys, or something?" Ellanece couldn't
help not hiding the demonic grin that she wore on
her face. "Dennis I have a slight confession to
make." Not really knowing how to respond, he
asked, "Okay, what's that?" Ellanece let a puckish
giggle escape, "My name isn't really Stella, I kinda
just made all that shit up." Confused and slightly
worried by the overly excited demeanor of
Ellanece's attitude, he slowly began to back up, and
asked, "It's not? Then what is it?"

"I'll put it to ya this way: My name's Ella,
and you're about to be *one dead fella*!" Ellanece
ripped open her counter drawer, where she snatched
up the massive meat cleaver which was soon to
become the very tool that ended Dennis's life.
Looking around frantically, he realized that

Ellanece had cornered him in the kitchen, and that his only options were begging for mercy, or charging her, not being too excited to run towards the giant meat cleaver, that she held in her hand, he began to beg. "Lady please, I don't know who you are? I don't care! Please just let me live, I don't want to die!"

"Look at my face and tell me, does it actually look like I care if you want to *die*, or not?" Ellanece swung the knife several times sometimes missing; other times whacking away chunks of clothing and flesh. Dennis tried dodging the strikes but just wound up shuffling around in a circle. They shuffled around so many times, that an opportunity arose, for Dennis to make a break for it, and when he took his shot, Ellanece, jumped up on him, wrapping her legs around his waist and delivered the cleaver into its final resting place, right in the middle of his skull.

She popped off his hips as he fell to the floor, blood spewed from his scalp, pooling into the cracks of the floorboards. Blood had spattered everywhere, including all over her, due all of the slashes and the final death blow. Ellanece took her finger, and wiped a splotch of blood off of her face, she held her finger up to the kitchen light, admiring the glistening red tint of the blood, and continued to stick that finger into her mouth, slurping away the blood that covered it.

It was about that time that she saw the flashing lights of the first responding officers, so she began to let out several blood curdling screams. Police entered with guns drawn, and Ellanece flung herself at them, perfectly executing the *damsel in distress* card. As they began to escort her out away from the traumatic scene of the dead body in her kitchen, she managed to reach into her linen closet, where she grabbed a white afghan to wrap around her as she waited for Detective Jasper Lewis to arrive for questioning.

Chapter III

An Open and Closed Murder Case

Detective Lewis pulled up outside of the residence of the late Dennis Henderson, where his land lord, Mr. Carlisle, a small framed elderly gentleman, who wore thick framed glasses, and a slight over bite, waited for him to arrive. The Detective was quick to get out of his cruiser, he couldn't wait to question Mr. Carlisle about the late Mr. Henderson's personal life.

As he approached the house his work phone buzzed with a text message from his partner, Detective Harmon: *WTF? R U leaving me off of the DH Case, because it involves a murder? If U think UR protecting me, by leaving me to sit here at the station, dealing with drugs and petty thefts, then UR dead wrong... this won't be the last U hear from me.* Lewis dismissed the text, not worrying himself with his rookie partner, and slipped the phone into his back pocket.

Aside from wanting to know about the daily runabouts of Henderson's life, he also wanted to find out if Mr. Carlisle knew of any next of kin, which might be able to clue him in on the deceased's personal background. As Lewis approached the Landlord, he stuck out his hand, and said, "Mr. Carlisle, I'm Detective Lewis. I hate we had to meet under these conditions, but it's a pleasure all the same."

As the two men shook hands, Mr. Carlisle replied, "Like wise." Lewis took a moment to take a really good look at the surroundings. The neighborhood wasn't bad, (but it wasn't great either). The house was your typical starter home, the type of place a young couple just starting out might be interested in buying. Wood framed, aluminum siding, with one car driveway.

Mr. Carlisle went to open the door, as the Detective continued to make his observations of the outside, as he was doing so, the towns church bells could be heard to alert the coming of a new hour "Are ya ready to see the place, Detective? I don't mean to rush; it's just I have to be somewhere at eleven o'clock."

"Yea sure, my bad. I assure you, Mr. Carlisle, this won't take any time at all. The two men entered the home; they made their way through the main hall way into the den, where Lewis noticed that the place was not as he imagined it would be. "It's…clean," he said, "Everything is very neat and tidy. I can't say I was expecting this at all." Mr.

Carlisle paused placing his hands on his hips and said, "Yup, Mr. Henderson ran a pretty tight ship. He is—I mean *was* one of the only tenants that I have ever had that actually kept up with the place; and wasn't calling me to fix something every time I turned around. Say, how exactly did Mr. Henderson die?"

Lewis shook his head and replied, "I'm not at liberty to say at the moment, all you really need to know is that he passed under such circumstances, that a Homicide Detective, like myself, is investigating his cause of death." Mr. Carlisle pushed his glasses up onto his face and said, "I see." Lewis continued to look around the place, until he found an item of great interest, a laptop, still up and running, sitting on a coffee table that was positioned in front of a couch.

The Detective made his was over to the couch, took a seat in front of the computer, and pulled up the last active page. The screen which was littered with e-mails between the deceased and a certain female, named *Tina*, whom Lewis had every reason to believe, was actually Ellanece. Seeing all that he needed for the moment, he shut the laptop, unplugged it, and wrapped the cord in a tight circle. "I'm gonna be confiscating this, for my official investigation. While I'm at it, you wouldn't happen to know what exactly it was, that Mr. Henderson did for a living, would you?"

"Oh yes sir, Mr. Henderson worked two jobs, actually. During the day he worked as a sales clerk, for Office Depot, and on weekends he worked as a waiter down at that little Italian restaurant, called *Mama Mia's*."

"Tell me Mr. Carlisle, are you aware of any *next of kin* that Mr. Henderson might have had?" Mr. Carlisle was very quick to answer, nodding very enthusiastically, "Oh yea, the man was real, I mean *real* close to his mother, Clara Woodberry." Lewis took an interest in the way that Mr. Carlisle had emphasized how close the deceased and his mother were. "How do you mean, *real* close, Mr. Carlisle?"

Once again pushing his glasses further up the bridge of his nose, he replied, "Well you see, Mr. Henderson has only rented from me for the past two years. Prior to that, I have no knowledge of him ever residing at any other place than at his mother's. Not to mention that his credit was in such bad shape that she had to co-sign on the lease with him. I'll even admit I was weary at first to even let him sign. But the guy pulled through, he made every payment on time, was never late, and like I said earlier, took really good care of the place, I'm actually kind of sad that he's gone."

"Other than living with his mother till he was thirty, did you find anything else odd about their relationship?"

"Nope, not really, I mean, other than the fact that she was over for dinner almost every night. Excluding the weekends, when he worked as a waiter of course. But I just figured the man couldn't cook, or maybe he just really enjoyed his momma's cooking. I never really thought too much about it, till just now." The Detective finished taking his notes and was quick to thank Mr. Carlisle for his time, and being so cooperative in letting him see the residence.

Detective Lewis headed straight for his cruiser, where he carefully placed the evidence that he had collected into his trunk. He then got into his car, and got on his work laptop, to look up the residence of Ms. Clara Woodberry. As the detective set course for his new destination, he got on his phone to let his Lieutenant know everything that he had found, Lewis heard three rings before Pogue picked up, "What ya got Lewis?"

"Not a whole lot, just finishing up here at Henderson's pad, found a laptop which had a shit tone of craigslist postings and internet porn on it. Other than that the landlord painted Henderson out to be a pretty quiet and normal guy; even quoted him as being *one of the best tenants he's ever had.* Anyways, I'm headed over to the deceased's mother's house, Clara Woodberry, to see if I can't squeeze anything out of her."

"Hey don't bother going to her home just yct, see if you can't meet her down by the morgue, she's supposed to be identifying the body today, if you hurry, you could still catch her."
Lewis rolled his window down and popped a flashing red gum-ball on the roof of his cruiser, and replied, "Appreciate the tip—headed there now."

"Oh yea one more thing, don't be surprised if Harmon meets you down there, she hasn't left me alone, for two minutes yammering on about how it's *so sexist* that you and I are excluding her from the murder case, and how if I don't let her assist you on the case, she's going to run to the internal affairs, for sexual discrimination." As Lewis blew through a red light trying to make good time he hesitantly asked, "Are you about to order me to let her assist?"

"Lewis I have enough confidence in you that you know what's best for this case, if you feel you can handle it better and faster without her, then send her ass back to HQ, but I'm warning ya, things will just go a hell of a lot smoother, if you just let her assist."

"Enough said. I hear ya boss, I'll handle it carefully, I gotta run though, catch ya later." Lewis, ended the call and tucked the phone back into his back pocket, continuing to drive as fast as he could, down to the morgue. When he first pulled up to the morgue, he was worried that he might have missed her. Other than two hearses, one white and one black, parked in the corner of the parking lot, there were only two vehicles other than his, one of the vehicles belonging to his pain in the ass partner, Traci Harmon.

Though he knew that it wasn't likely that he was going to find the mother, he figured he could at least see if the receptionist could tell him how long she had stayed, and if she gave any hints as to where she may be going next. The two Detectives exited out of their vehicles in a synchronized manner, almost as if they had rehearsed it a hundred times.

"I'm helping you conduct this investigation whether you like it or not!" Harmon exclaimed. Lewis rounded the front of his cruiser and when he got to Harmon, he gently, yet firmly placed both of his hands on her shoulders and said, "I don't know who the hell it is you think you are, but you better take your ass back to the station, *now*!" Bumping his hands off of her, Harmon replied, "This is bullshit and you know it! Just because I'm a woman—"

"—Let me stop you right there, Harmon! You want to go into how this department is comprised of a bunch of sexist assholes; you're right! The only reason you got promoted to Detective, was because you're a female! I know of at least two other male Officers that would have made a better Detective then you, so you wanna go grumble to the Lieutenant, Captain, or IAD, about sexism, you go right the hell ahead. Go on, get!"

Without saying another word, Lewis turned his back, and began to make his way into the morgue. Harmon, not knowing exactly how she should handle what had just happened, sluggishly got back into her car and drove away.

When Lewis entered through the large black doors accented with gold handles, he was greeted by a pretty young lady in a pink dress with blonde hair and green eyes. "Hi there Detective, how may I help you today?" asked the young woman. "Mornin' Cindy, I was wondering if you could tell me if anybody's stopped by, to claim the body of Dennis Henderson?"

Cindy batted her eyelashes, and replied, "Yes sir, his mother stopped by about half an hour ago; I think she's still in there. She was mighty distressed, and asked if she could have a moment with her son? I told her she could take as long as she needed." Surprised to hear the news, he asked to reconfirm, "You mean Ms. Clara Woodberry is still here?" the young lady's skinny red lips tightened and she bobbed her head showing sympathy for the grieving mother. The Detective pointed down the hall, and the young woman responded, "Yes sir, second door on your right."

Lewis entered into the room where he was told the deceased and his mother would be, and as he entered the room he was met by a grieving woman, leaning over her son's body, gently stroking his once half split forehead. "Oh Denny, Denny, Denny, what on earth have you gotten yourself into?" the mother wept. Hating to interrupt, Lewis cleared his throat to make his presence known, and said, "Excuse me ma'am, I'm Detective Jasper Lewis, and I am more than willing to help answer any questions that you may have about your son's death, just as long as you are willing to answer my questions about his life."

The mother shot up from her son, and quickly made her way over to Lewis with tears streaming down her face, "Who's the rotten sonofabitch that did this to my boy? Please tell me you got him, or at least know where to find him?"

Not knowing exactly how he was going to break the news to the grief-stricken woman, Lewis gently placed his hands on her shoulders, and said, "Ma'am if you would, please come over here, and have a seat. I'll inform you as best I can, of how your son wound up in this current situation."

The two walked over to the far right wall of the room where they both took a seat, all the woman could do was sniffle, and try her best to wipe all of the tears from her cheek. Feeling sorry for the woman, Lewis reached down into his pants and pulled out a folded bandana, and handed it over to the woman, "It's clean," he said. The woman took his bandana, and wiped her tears off of her face. She then looked to the Detective, and with the sorriest eyes he ever set eyes on, she asked from the bottom of her heart, "What happened to my boy?"

Gently placing a hand on the woman's shoulder, he began to tell her, "Mrs. Hend—I beg your pardon, *Ms. Woodberry*, I know that it's no mother's business to know the personal life of her son, and by personal I mean the life he led in the bedroom, behind closed doors. But, how familiar are you with the women that your son dated/fooled around with?"

Ms. Woodberry was quick to bring her hand up to her mouth, she then looked to Lewis, as a few more tears escaped from her eye, "So it was his *addiction* that did him in?" Puzzled by what the woman had just said, he asked, "*Addiction?*" shaking her head Ms. Woodberry asked, "How much money did he owe this time?" shrugging his shoulders, Lewis replied, "Money? Ma'am, your son didn't owe anyone, any money. Your son was killed, after he responded to a Craigslist personals ad." Clara's eyes shut tight as she now brought both hands up to cover her mouth to try and keep from making a scene.

After taking a few moments to regain her composure she asked, "Was it a trap? Ya know, one of those deals, where after he shows up, he's jumped by six or seven people who just want to get his wallet from him?" Not able to tell if the woman was still in shock and denial, or if she was really just that naïve, Lewis responded, "Ma'am, when we recovered your son's body he was still in possession of all of his personal belongings, including his wallet which had not been touched."

The woman's brow furrowed in confusion as she tried to think of another possible scenario, "Do you think he might have been the victim of an angered spouse?" Lewis once again shook his head, "No ma'am the female that he visited was single, and we also have reason to believe that he wasn't the victim." Realizing what the detective was trying to tell her she asked not knowing if she wanted to hear the answer, "You mean the woman killed him out of self-defense?"

Lewis nodded, "Ms. Woodberry, I'm afraid that I can't really go into that many more details with you on the case right now. But, I am curious; you seem to have prior knowledge of your sons, *personal life* you've even mentioned an *addiction*. I hate to ask you this question, but is it possible that Dennis was a sex addict?"

Ms. Woodberry closed her eyes once again, slowly nodding her head, "It first started when he was a teenager. I would be cleaning his room and would stumble upon magazines like *Playboy* and *Hustler*. I was of coarse disturbed and upset at first, but I figured *boys will be boys* and that it was only natural for a young man to want to look at naked women.

"But as he got older, the magazines just got dirtier and dirtier. More *hardcore* as the kids call it; magazines like *Swank* and *Naughty Surprise*. The magazines turned into DVDs, which later turned into hookers. It wasn't until after one of his *girlfriends* threatened to press rape charges against him, after he tried to sodomize her during sex, that's when I knew that he needed help."

Lewis was quick to throw a finger up and interrupt, "So Dennis does in fact have a history of rape?" slapping his finger down, Ms. Woodberry, was quick to her son's defense, "Not rape! It was attempted sodomy, and for Christ's sake they were already doing it! He just went a little *too* far over the line, that's all."

"I believe sodomy classifies as going much further than just a little over the line." Replied Lewis. Clara shook her head, dismissing his last statement and continued, "We settled with the family outside of court, and that is when I had him start going to Sex Addicts Anonymous meetings."

"Which group does he meet at?"

"Well originally, he met at the local AA club house for SAA meetings. He was doing really well for a while there, he even started sponsoring others, I was so proud of him, for overcoming his disease. Because that's what addiction is, ya know? It's a goddamned disease!" Rolling his eyes, Lewis asked, "So if I go to this AA club house, who should I ask for, about how your son was handling his *disease*?"

Ms. Woodberry shook her head once more, "No one. You see, after several years of attendance, and mentoring…he relapsed. He had sexual relations with several of the female members in the group, and was banned. He spent the next couple of years, bouncing around from group to group; every now and then he would admit to me that he relapsed.

"One of the times that he relapsed, he needed to borrow some money. He had fallen into debt with a particular escort service. However, for the past two years he has been attending a group at Bucksdale Baptist Church. The group is being counseled by a Dr. John Carroll. He could probably tell you anything and everything that you needed to know about Dennis and his addiction."

Trying his best to act concerned and appear sincere with the woman, Lewis put an arm around Ms. Woodberry's shoulder, as he could see how hard she was trying to hold back her tears. "Thank you so much for your cooperation Ms. Woodberry. You have been a lot of help. I truly am sorry about your loss. If it's any comfort to you, I went to school with your son, and though I—we never really hung out, or talked much, due to me being two grades above him. We did share one PE class; I could tell that he was a really nice guy. I hate that things had to end the way that they did."

Lewis tried to stand up, but was surprised when Ms. Woodberry latched on to him, giving him one of the biggest hugs he had received in a long while. She only hugged him for a moment, and when she was done, she said with all of her heart, "Thank you Detective, for handling the case like a human being, and not some drone government official. It means a lot to me that you and my son attended school together." Lewis nodded to Ms. Woodberry, giving her goodbye salute, and made his way out of the room.

Lewis was shocked to find out that the stiff known as Dennis Henderson actually had an extensive background in sexual addiction. This made Ellanece's story sound all the more plausible. The next day the Detective pulled up outside of the Bucksdale Baptist Church, hoping to be able to talk with Dr. John Carroll. When he first entered he was taken by how modern the place looked.

In his childhood, he had been raised with a Baptist back ground, and had actually attended the Bucksdale Baptist Church. However, it had been many years since he had even the slightest thoughts of entering into a house of God. Also, the original Church was one of the oldest churches in the town of Bucksdale, unfortunately, a few years' prior; an F5 tornado had blown through, demolishing the original building which had been established in 1870. As he walked through the new modern halls of the church, to try and find someone who might know where he could find Dr. Carroll, the modern architecture of the building really messed with some of his old memories of the place.

He eventually found his way to the preacher, Harry Powell, who was sitting in his office. The door was open and he could see the pastor silently doing work at his desk. He was an elderly plump gentleman, with feathered white hair, which was fluffiest up top, but flattened out along the sides and back of his head.

As he approached, he knocked on the door frame, "Pastor Powell, I was wondering if you could spare just a moment of your time, to help me try and locate someone?" Slightly startled, the Pastor grabbed his glasses, and put them on, as he winced to see who he was talking to. "Well, well, well, Jasper Lewis, it's been a minute. 'Bout the last time I saw you must've been 'round—March of last year I suppose." Lewis nodded and stated, "Sounds 'bout right. Look sir, as much as I would love to stand around and receive a guilt trip, about how it's been a year and a half since I set foot in this place, all I's need from you is to know where I can find Dr. John Carroll."

The Pastor leaned back into his chair, scratching his chin and asked, "You having some personal problems there, son? You do know what kind of doctor he is, right?" All that Lewis could do was roll his eyes while shaking his head, "No sir, I don't need to speak with him for me. The doctor may be able to enlighten me on a certain case that I am working on."

The Pastor leaned towards his desk, resting his large round arms on it, stating, "Ah! Well, I'm afraid he is only here, three afternoons out of the week. Luckily for you, today, just so happens to be one of the afternoons that he holds a meeting here. If you plan on talking to him today, you might as well just wait around here. His meetings are held in room 2B." The Pastor smiled, and then continued back to his work, Lewis cracked a smile as he walked away, couldn't help but chuckle over how all Baptist Ministers are all the same."

Dr. Carroll fumbled his way into the meeting room, trying to balance his briefcase, along with the fast food that he had brought with him. When he flicked on the lights, he was met by an unexpected visitor; Detective Lewis, who sat in one of the chairs organized into a circle for the SAA meetings. "Dr. John Carroll I presume. I'm Detective Lewis, and I would like to ask you a few questions about one the regulars in your meetings."

"Oh Lord," the doctor said in a very whiny and nasally southern accent, "who's done what now?" Lewis got up from his seat and said, "I hate to be the bearer of bad news, but it's about Dennis Henderson." The Doctor dropped everything that he was holding out of shock and disbelief, "Oh no, not Dennis! What's happened?"

Lewis once again found himself not knowing where to begin, "Well sir, Mr. Henderson, was killed the other night, at the scene of what I now suspect to be, an attempted raping." The Doctors jaw instantly dropped, "Rape? That doesn't sound like Dennis at all. He was always such a mild-mannered young man."

"That's what I wanted to talk to you about." Lewis replied, "Now, I didn't know the man well, but I have known of him ever since we both attended school together. He never seemed to display those characteristics to me either. On the other hand, I talked with his mother yesterday morning, and she revealed that a little over ten years ago, he attempted to sodomize a woman during sex. She almost pressed a rape charge against him because he wanted to try anal sex against her will."

The Doctor was now pacing the room, softly tapping his chin with his index finger, "Well that's an addict for you, Detective. The only predictable thing about them is that they are unpredictable. Even the nicest of *nice* possess a devil deep inside of them, a demon that could erupt at a moment's notice. I take it Mr. Henderson responded to an internet personal's ad?" puzzled at how remarkably close the Doctor was, Lewis replied, "Yes, how did you know?"

The Doctor twisted his mouth while nodding his head, "Let's just say a doctor knows his patients, Detective. And I consider every soul that steps into this room looking for help, a patient. Finding partners over the internet, just so happened to be Mr. Henderson's MO."

"So you're saying that even though Mr. Henderson could have been the nicest guy in the world—say *the situation* was he answered a post for some no strings attached sex, once he arrived to the booty call; she got a case of cold feet, and told him to leave. You're saying that it is possible for *Mr. Nice Guy* to unleash this—*devil* inside, which would cause him to act out such a heinous act of rape?"

The Doctor simply nodded, "Yes Detective, that's what I'm saying. The tragedy of it all is that after committing this heinous act, knowing his temperament, and character, he would most likely have hated himself for it. Especially a guy like Dennis, he may even loath himself so much, that it would drive him to the point of suicide. So I suppose it's just as well, that whoever did him in, did it before he could do it himself."

The Detective had heard everything that he needed to hear, he was now convinced more than ever, that Ellanece's story indeed checked out, and that she was innocent of any murder charge. All she had done was protected herself, from being raped.

As he left the church he intended on stopping by Ellanece's place, to deliver the news that he found her innocent and that she would have nothing to worry about, once she appeared in court, but later decided that it could wait until the following day. Though he hated to admit that a guy like Dennis could commit such a terrible crime, he was somewhat relieved that such a little southern lady, as charming as Ellanece, was not capable of cold-blooded murder.

He was a little more than anxious, the next day as he walked up the rickety old steps to Ellanece's home. He walked up to the door, and could hear her rummaging around inside, busy with what sounded like the sounds of a little bit of hard labor. He gave three loud knocks, hoping that she would be able to hear them over all of the racket.

Sure enough all of the commotion from inside came to a sudden halt, and it wasn't long before the old faded door, slowly opened. "Detective Lewis; what brings you here?" wiping away a half crooked smile he replied, "Oh you know, just the usual, following up on a little murder investigation. You mind if I come in, so that we may talk a little more privately? Not to mention it would be nice to get out of all this heat." Ellanece swung her door wide open and motioned for him to enter.

Ellanece slowly shut the door behind them. The Detective tried to crack a joke and said, "Ya know, I don't think I like how eerily slow you closed that door. That's the type of things you see in horror movies, with houses like these." Ellanece chuckled and shook her head, "Oh Detective, don't be so silly. This is an old place, with old appendages; you gotta be gentle with a place like this." Lewis cocked his head to the side and winced at her, and said, "I been doing a little digging the past couple of days, anyway long story short, do to some uncovering's I've convinced prosecutors to drop any and all murder charges against you."

She quickly covered her mouth with her hands, to try and cover her gasp, Detective Lewis nodded, and continued on, "Turns out a little over ten years ago, he tried raping one of his girlfriends—and well, beforehand we had no knowledge of this event, because, charges had never been filed."

Ellanece was shocked, to find out about Dennis Henderson's previous rape attempt. This was a detail that she knew absolutely nothing about, originally her plan had just been to find a guy with a record of sexual addiction, and use that as her alibi for murdering him. She knew the police were going to have their questions, she also accounted that she would most likely be charged with murder, she had even expected the authorities to do some prodding. But having Mr. Henderson's prior rape fall right into her lap, giving her the perfect cover up was something that had come right out of the blue. Now all she had to do was put on her southern charm and act as normal as possible.

"Well Ms. Mosley, I really must be on my way. I just wanted to stop by so that I could ease your mind, and possibly even save you the trouble and money of thinking you needed a lawyer. I just hope you realize that it was nothing personal, ya know, seeing as how you're from Alabama and all. Honestly, I really was just doing my job, no matter how unpleasant it can be at times." Ellanece smiled and nodded her head, "I completely understand Detective."

She came to a pause and smiled at Lewis, making it a point to show her shiny white teeth, "I Just hate you had to arrest me and all, I mean after all, a girl's gotta reputation to up hold, and here I am being all new and what not, getting hauled off for questioning in my first six months here. People talk ya know!"

Lewis placed a hand on her shoulder and said; "Well ma'am, ya did it to yourself, hittin' up strange dudes on the internet, it's only a recipe for disaster. You're a very beautiful young woman— you should have no trouble at all finding you a strapping young man, with manners, an education, and a means to provide for ya. All this going around knocking boots with strangers from the internet, is a sure fire way to get people to talking."

Ellanece batted her eyes towards Lewis, "All's I'm sayin' is maybe you could make it up to me by taking me out to dinner some time? You look pretty strapping to me, with that chiseled jaw, broad shoulders, and ripped arms."

Lewis took a few steps back and said, "Jesus! There ain't no messing around with you *Bama-girls*, is there? Y'all jump straight to the point. Also, hitting back on the subject of people talking, I'm pretty sure a detective taking out his former lead murder suspect, in his recently closed case, where he found the said suspect, innocent. Might sound pretty fishy to some folks.

"So as much as I hate to decline, there's just no way we can see each other. As a matter of fact, we really shouldn't even entertain the idea of becoming friends even. I'm afraid the only kind of relationship we can have, is a professional one. Where I am just a civil servant providing a service as lawman, to you the citizen." Lewis began to make his way towards the door, "Now like I said earlier ma'am, I closed my case, you're off the hook, and my business with you is now done. I hope you enjoy the rest of your day." Lewis brought two fingers up to his brow to salute good bye, and continued to exit the home.

Chapter IV

The Illegal Help

Ellanece was still in the process of remodeling her home at 300 East Church Street. It had been a month and a half since the Henderson Case had been closed, and she had put a little bit of dent in doing most of the work on the house herself, nonetheless there were still times when she came across a job that would require more muscle or more expertise than she had to offer; so in order to cheaply compensate for her lack of skill or knowledge, she would get in her Firebird and drive down to the local co-op and recruit an illegal immigrant or two, to help her out.

She only dealt with *illegals* when it came to needing help (mainly because they worked for such little pay.) One day, as her progress in the home moved to her kitchen, she found that she was in need of some new cabinets, so she figured she would hire a Hispanic from the co-op, her plan was to offer him more than enough cash up front, and after the cabinets were installed, she would kill the man and get her cash back. The next morning, she drove down to the co-op around eight in the morning.

By the time she arrived, all that was left were the straggler rejects who were just too desperate to return home empty handed. As Ellanece pulled her Firebird into the parking lot, she maneuvered the vehicle into a position so that she could gaze upon the rejects to make the choice of which man would become her next victim; she instantly noticed a skinny dark brown colored man with a staid look on his face. He was sitting with his knees drawn up to his chest, with his arms folded on top.

Ellanece got out of her car and as she approached the remaining men, she called out, "Buenos dias, señors. Necesito dos hombres para ayudarme a instalar algunos gabinetes de la cocina." All of the men naturally, eagerly jumped up from where they had been sitting or crouching, and raised their hands in the air, exclaiming things like, "¡Soy un hombre muy trabajador que pueda realizar el trabajo!"

It didn't matter who said what, Ellanece had already chosen her two men. "Usted ahí," she called out, pointing to the dark brown colored man with the composed face, "¿Como te llames?" The man stuck his finger in his chest asking, "¿Quién mí?" Ellanece replied, "¡Sí!" the man's face lit up and he exclaimed, "¡Vicente!" Ellanece smiled, simultaneously batting her eyes and waving him over, while saying, "Ven conmigo Vicente, tengo llegado emplear tus servicios."

Excited to have been chosen, Vicente went back to where he had been siting and picked up his tool belt, and tool box. Ellanece then pointed to another man who was very short in stature but stocky with thick arms, she pointed him, "Y su nombre es?"

The man kicked his feet in the dirt, replying, "Gustavo." Ellanece shrugged replying, "Si desea que el trabajo, que es la suya." Thinking to himself, not being as eager to accept, as Vicente had been, he inquired, "¿Cuánto estás pagando?" to which Ellanece rolled her eyes, "Vamos a hablar de eso mas tarde. Yo tienes tu dinero. ¿Eres conmigo, sí o no?" Gustavo reluctantly nodded his head, "Sí quiero el trabajo."

As Ellanece and her new hired help got into her car and drove off, Ellanece looked over to Vicente and asked, "¿Habla Inglés?" Vicente replied, "I do. I was actually just about to ask you the same thing." Vicente's witty response caused Ellanece to genuinely laugh out loud. She then looked to Gustavo, "¿Y tu?" the man shook his head no, replying, "No. Sólo hablo de una pequeña cantidad—only basic íngles." Ellanece grimaced, mumbling under her breath, "Two words is a little less than basic."

Vicente placed a hand on her shoulder, "There shouldn't be any problem. You seem to know your español and I speak fairly decent English, so we shouldn't have any communication issues." Forcing a smile, Ellanece stated, "No, there won't be any problem at all—I just hate switching back and forth between the two languages. But it'll have to work I suppose.

"So here's the deal: Everything I'm about to tell you, you can retell your friend, in the back: I'm remodeling a home on the other side of town, and all I really need is to have the old cabinets in the kitchen removed, and have the new ones installed;

you think you two can get that done in a day's time?"

Vicente thought for a moment calculating all of the labor that would need to be done, squinting he shrugged, "Eh, I suppose, I've never worked with this man before, so I don't truly know his work ethic, but I'll give him the benefit of the doubt. If it's a typical kitchen with typical cabinets, then we should be able to get it done today."

Ellanece cleared her throat and said, "$500 bucks. *In cash*, if you are able to complete the job, today." Tucking his chin into his chest, wincing at the beautiful young woman, Vicente inquired, "Each?" Without skipping a beat, Ellanece scoffed, "Fuck no! You two will split it however ya'll see fit.

Badly needing all the cash, Vicente inquired "—the new cabinets, they are—pre fabricado, derecho?"

"Oh yea, of course they are. Asking you to tear down old cabinets, so you can build new ones from scratch, and install them all in one day is just ludicrous." She chortled. Smiling with a sigh of relief Vicente stated, "I do not mean to come off as a dishonest man, but I'm in some real need of money.

"Would it bother you if I told the guy in the back that we were only getting paid one hundred-fifty each for the job, so that I could keep the majority of the pay?" Ellanece shrugged, I don't give a shit what you tell him; as long as the goddamn job gets done by the end of the day." Ellanece smiled and winked at Vicente as the wind from the rolled down windows whipped her hair all around her face.

They arrived at Ellanece's home, pulling into the drive way at the back of the property. As the three of them got out of the car and walked around front, the entire time, Ellanece explained, "Yea, so I purchased this old gal at a bargain of a price, only me and one other lady, I think that she might have been a cop, I don't know for sure, she just had an air about her; anyways, she just didn't have the funds that she thought she needed, to get the place.

"It's a real fixer upper, but I think I can make a decent profit off of it, if I finish her up in a timely manner." The three entered in through the front door, Vicente stopping at it, rubbing his hands up and down it, and said, "Your door is in very bad need of replacing." To which Ellanece replied, "Yea, all of 'em need to be." Continuing to check the door out, he knocked on it, with the back of his knuckle, and said, "After I finish with your cabinets, if you are satisfied with my work, I could return and replace all of your doors for you." Nodding, she replied, "I think we can work something out."

Ellanece waved them in, and continued to show them where the kitchen was, and as they entered she pointed to the far left corner where she had a mound of supplies and pre-manufactured cabinets stacked up, and she said, "There, y'all should have all of the materials that you need, if you find that y'all are out, or can't find anything, just let me know and I'll go run to the hardware store and get it for you."

Vicente looked to Gustavo saying, "Vamosa llegar a ella, me ayudan a empezar a tomar todos los antiguos gabinetes de abajo." The two men worked all through the day taking the old cabinets down trying to be careful not to damage the wall. They both found themselves honestly surprised when one o'clock rolled around and Ellanece walked in with a to-go-meal from *Arby's*, "Got ya'll the same thing," she said, "if you don't like it, ya don't have to eat it, I just thought that ya'll been working so hard that ya'll might've gotten hungry."

She dropped the bag on the counter and without saying another word, walked out of the kitchen, returning to the chores that she had set aside for herself, for the day. She did the same thing around dinner; ordering a large pizza, and giving them half of it.

After they scarfed down their dinner, they diligently returned to work, working all through the evening all the way up until eight o'clock that night. As she was finishing up one of her projects, she was about to go and tell the two illegals that they would just have to stop and return for work the next day, when she heard Vicente yell out from the kitchen, "Señorita we're through, come have a look see, to see if we have met your expectations."

Ellanece stopped what she was doing and made her way down the stairs, upon entering the kitchen, she was legitimately impressed with the work that they had done. Nodding her head, she reached into her bra to retrieve the cash and as soon as Vicente saw the green of the cash he put his arm around the woman, and looked to his partner, informing, "Espera quí, mientras yo colecciono nuestro dinero." He then looked to Ellanece muttering in her ear, "Remember our arrangement, mind if I receive that money in the other room?" Sliding the cash back into her cleavage, she replied, winking, "Right. Sorry, I almost forgot."

The two made their way into the other room and Ellanece once again removed the cash handing him the money, stating, "Hey, I don't blame you for holding out on your partner. I mean shit, after all it's his fault for not knowing English, right."

Vicente motioned for her to tone her voice down, informing, "He knows a little. Basic stuff, like: Introductions, basic directions, and numbers— well up to a certain point, anyways." Contorting her face, she hissed, "My bad! So I'm guessing I only need to give you guys a ride back to the co-op, or do y'all need rides all the way home?" Vicente pocketed away his share of the cash, replying, "We are both staying at the Minx-Winx motel, if you don't mind, think you could drop us both off there?" Ellanece smiled, "Sure thing."

The two reentered the kitchen where Gustavo still stood. Vicente held out his hand containing the man's shaved pay for the day. "Aquí esta tus sueldo." Gustavo accepted the money, and as he counted it, he replied, "¿Esto es todo dinero?" Vicente nodded, "Sí, amigo." Gustavo walked right up to Ellanece and said, "*Cheap bitch.*" Vicente reached out and pulled his coworker back. Ellanece cut a look to Gustavo, then to Vicente, and stated,

"So we're through here?" Vicente nodded his head, "Sí."

Ellanece looked around to all the scattered tools and materials, and asked, "So about how long till you guys get all your tools gathered, and the old cabinets moved to the side of the road?" Vicente shrugged, "Whoa wait a minute, you want us haul all that shit to the side of the road too? That wasn't a part of the original deal?"

Grinding her teeth together, she commanded, "Move this shit out of my house, or I make my new mission in life to get you and your buddy deported!" recognizing the dreaded *D* word Gustavo inquired, "¿*Deportados*?" Vicente raised a hand to calm the man, then turned his attention back to his employer, "Okay, I'll do it. But I cannot ask him to help. I've cheated the guy out of enough as it is."

Turning to his coworker once again, Vicente instructed, "Permanecer aquí mientras me deshago de los viejos gabinetes." Gustavo shrugged, "¿Ese no es nuestro trabajo?" cutting his eyes to Ellanece, he replied, "Sí, es mi trabajo, no nuestros." While Vicente traveled back and forth removing the old cabinets and debris, Gustavo stayed inside, and collected the tools. Every now and then, Ellanece would enter the kitchen, with her iPhone in hand, taking photos of the newly installed cabinets. As she did so, she couldn't help but notice, Gustavo, cutting dirty looks at her from time to time.

Putting her phone away, she walked over to him, while Vicente was out of the room, carrying the old cabinets to the side of the road, and asked,

"¿Cuál es tu problema conmigo, y por qué me has llamado barato?" Getting in her face he exclaimed, "¡Porque, tu sólo nos pagó ciento cincuenta dólares por todo el trabajo duro!" Ellanece covered her mouth acting as if she was shocked, and explained to the man that she had no idea, that Vicente, had cheated him out of one hundred dollars. That she had handed Vicente five hundred dollars for the two of them to split evenly.

Gustavo scratched his head, not sure if he could trust what the *gringa* was telling him, "¡No te creo!" he elated. Upon hearing the man confess that he didn't believe her, she instructed him to check Vicente, once he returned from the outside. As he entered the kitchen, wiping sweat from his brow, he couldn't help but noticed the two dead-eying him, "¿Qué?" Vicente inquired. Gustavo looked to Ellanece then back to Vicente, and shrugged as if nothing was the matter.

Ellanece looked to Vicente, with a straight poker face, and stated, "Nothing is the matter. Just get the rest of this shit out of here. Rolling his eyes, Vicente made his way over to the last of the trash, that he was to take out and as he bent over to pick it up, Gustavo reached over and snatched the wallet out of his back pocket. Vicente jumped up to try and retrieve the wallet from his coworker, but Gustavo was too fast, and ripped the cash out and after counting the money he inquired, "¿Por qué demonios hacer tu tengo un extra de cien dólares en su billetera maldito, hijo de puta?"

Vicente looked to Ellanece, pissed that she had ratted him out to his coworker. He then continued to explain that he had had the extra hundred since the beginning of the day. Upon hearing the lame explanation, Gustavo said, "¡*Mierda*!" Vicente cut his eyes to Ellanece and questioned, "What the hell? I thought we had an understanding?" To which Gustavo questioned, "*Understanding*, qué quiere decir que tenía ella una comprensión?"

Ellanece could see the rage growing in his eyes, as he switched looks from her to Vicente. Gesturing with her hands, she explained, "Whoa, it's not like that—¡Que no es así!" Looking to his employer Gustavo yelled, "You dead bitch!" He then turned toward Vicente elating, "¡Usted es muerto también, hijo de puta!" He then charged towards Ellanece, she tried to escape, but Gustavo was too fast for her, as he tackled her to the ground. On her back, she had managed to pull her legs up to her chest, separating her body from his. However, that hadn't stopped him from getting a firm grip on her throat.

Unable to breathe, Ellanece's pretty pink lips had started to turn blue. Vicente stepped over Gustavo and pulled him off of her, which turned into the two men wrestling around on the floor trying to out maneuver the other one. By the time Ellanece had regained the ability to take full deep breaths, allowing her natural color to return. It had come to her attention the racket from the two men wrestling around had died down: *I wonder if they both made a run for it*? She thought to herself.

While grappling each other for control, the two had managed to make tussle into the next room.

Staggering to her feet, she made her way to the doorway and as she peaked into the next room, she saw both of the men lying on the floor. Vicente had managed to get Gustavo into a sleeper hold.

The only problem with that was that Gustavo's eyes had rolled into the back of his head, his lips were dark purple, and Vicente still hadn't let go. "I think he's out." She spoke hoarsely. Upon hearing her words of enlightenment, Vicente let go and as he did so, Gustavo's head thudded against the hard wood flooring. Vicente made his way to his feet, after he gathered himself together he looked to Ellanece then down to the floor where his fallen coworker laid.

He nudged Gustavo with his foot demanding, "¡Leventarse, hijo de puta!" Ellanece just shook her head, as she continued to rub her throat, saying, "I don't think he can get up?" Vicente looked to them woman then back down to the floor. A cold sweat broke at his brow, "What, like you mean he is passed out?" Vicente inquired. Once again shaking her head, she corrected, "No, more like he's dead—¡*Muerta*!"

Dropping to his knees, he covered his mouth with one hand while he checked Gustavo's pulse, with the other. "¡*Nooo!*" He hissed. He looked back to Ellanece, with tears streaming down his cheeks, "No,no,no—this cannot be—¡Yo no soy un asesino!" Smacking her lips, she replied, "Yea, try telling that shit to *ole boy* right there." A silence passed, finally being broke, with Vicente, wiping his wet brown cheeks, "My life is over. I have failed my family. I am going to be arrested now and sentenced for life. I was supposed to be *El Salvador* to my familia back home. They depended on me, and here I've gone, just like always, fucking shit up."

Ellanece made her way behind him, gently placing her hand on his shoulder, stating, "You know, it's just as bad for me, as it is for you, if this body gets found by the police." Pushing her hand away, he inquired, "Oh yea, and just how exactly is it *as bad* for you as it is for me? You're not the one who's killed any—"

"—This time!" She curtly interrupted. Vicente winced, looking back at her, "By what do you mean, *This Time*?" Ellanece rolled her eye as she sighed, "Look, a few months back a guy was over here, he tried to rape me and I kilt him…It was self defense, my right hand to God. However, it's still under investigation and another body popping up at my house just isn't gonna look right. They'll have me pegged as a serial killer for sure. So really, it behooves us both, if that body were to just disappear—I mean, for fuck's sake the dude barely spoke any English. I don't think anyone here is going to be missing him."

Vicente shook his head, "Maybe not here, but eventually, his people from back home will be missing him and will start searching for him, getting the authorities involved." Shrugging off the man's concern, Ellanece stated, "So? The dude, much like yourself, is here, illegally. Anyone wants to go asking about his whereabouts, is a damn fool, if they try to do so, by going through the proper authorities. Even if the cops do agree to help, him being here illegally, will put him low on their priorities list."

"So what is it exactly that you are suggesting? That we just wrap the body up and bury it somewhere?"

"*Bury him*—shit you're thinking way too damn hard. I mean even if we was to dig him a shallow grave it would take us half of the night." Vicente shrugged, "Then what is it you propose we do?"

"I once dated a guy, who was a real outdoorsman, I mean, *huge* hunter. Anyways, long story short, he once told me that feral hogs would eat anything—even human corpses. I say we load ole dude up in the back hatch of my car, make a stop by Emmet's Outdoor Expo, where I'll pick up a *hog bomb,* or whatever the fuck it was, my ex used to say would attract those things. Then we'll make our way out to the National Forrest where I'm pretty sure there's bound to be some hogs. We dump the body, ignite the pig grenade over the man's body and get the hell out of dodge."

Vicente once again exchanged looks between Ellanece and the body on the floor, "Are you sure it will work?" Ellanece shrugged, rolling her eyes, "Hell no I'm not sure. Nothing in life is guaranteed. However, it's the best thing I got to roll with, if you have something better, then please share." Vicente rubbed his hand through his thick jet black hair, "¿No lo sé? It was self-defense, you know. He said he was going to kill us both, he almost strangled you to death. What if we just went to the police and explained what happened?"

Ellanece shook her head no, "Like I said earlier, I can't have another body showing up at this house, whether someone else did it or not. Plus, both of you are illegal immigrants, there's no telling how they would treat the case. They could send you to jail just for being in the country illegally. Trust me. My way is the best option." Vicente thought for a moment, his thoughts of his family back home being the main catalyst behind his decision to follow through with Ellanece's plan.

Ellanece gestured towards the body on the floor; Vicente went for the torso while she grabbed the legs and with the help of the night's cover, they shuffled their way out of the house to the back of Ellanece's Firebird. It was a tight fit, but after much cramming and bone breaking, they were able to get Gustavo's corpse all the way into the back hatch of the vehicle.

The two made their way back into the house, as they entered through the front door, Ellanece commanded, "Gather your shit, we gotta hurry if we're gonna make it to Emmet's Outdoor Expo, before they close." Ellanece went upstairs where she collected her purse and her favorite pink polymer Taurus .380. Meanwhile, downstairs, Vicente collected the full five hundred dollars in cash, along with the rest of his tools.

Once Ellanece made it down with her purse, Vicente stated, "I'm keeping the full five-hundred." Ellanece nodded, "Sure thing hon. In fact, I was gonna give you an extra two hundred for helping me bury your buddy out there." Without any hesitation, Vicente insisted, "No. I want another five."

Ellanece quickly tossed her hand up, "Wait just a goddamn minute, how the hell you gonna ask for five hundred extra dollars, when I'm already helping you cover a murder *which you committed*?" Wiggling his finger with a wry smile, he replied, "Ah, ah, ah—I may have murdered someone in this house, and from the sounds of it, you have taken someone's life in this house too. Precisely why you don't want me going to the cops...You're paying me for my silence."

Ellanece thought for a moment, then inquired, "And if I don't give you the extra five?" Vicente shrugged, "Then we are done here, and I walk away. That leaves you to dispose of the body all on your own."

She threw her arms out exclaiming, "What the fuck? I can't move that dead bastard by myself?" Vicente smiled, "Not my problem, puta." Grimacing as she dug through her purse looking for her wallet, she muttered, "Sonofabitch, get 'em across the border and it's like they transform into goddamn capitalists overnight."

Hearing the woman's grumbles, Vicente chortled out loud, "Don't be mad, Señorita. After all, *it's the gringo way*!" She whipped out five crisp one hundred dollar bills, saying, "Here's your damn money! We best be on our way, if we're gonna pull this bitch off."

They pulled into the parking lot of Emmet's Outdoor Expo just as one of the employees was about to hang the closed sign. Ellanece ran, trotting up to the man with her right arm raised, pleading, "Please sir, let us in. We'll be quick I promise." The employee shook his head, "Sorry ma'am, we're closing!" Ellanece angrily pointed a finger to the hours sign, exclaiming, "Oh for fuck's sake! Y'all don't close till nine and it's only eight-fifty! I swear to God, just let us in real quick and we'll be gone before nine I swear it."

The employee, still unsure of what his next move should be, still shook his head no, trying to think of a valid excuse, to turn the crazed woman away, "I don't know ma'am—" Ellanece ripped her iPhone out, stating, "You really want me getting on the phone with Mr. Emmet, telling him he's just lost a loyal customer, all because his shit stain of an employee wouldn't let me in?"

Quickly changing his tune, he flipped the sign back around to open, saying, "No ma'am, that's not necessary. And welcome, to Emmet's Outdoor Expo, where we've got you covered, no matter where nature calls you." Ellanece rolled her eyes and huffed as she walked passed the store employee, Vicente, who was right behind her just gave the employee a silent cold stare. Walking down the isles to find the hog bomb, Ellanece had spoken of earlier.

Once they arrived at their desired location, she grabbed a can of the Hog Bomb and examined it closely making sure it was indeed the item she was looking for. "Are you sure that is all we'll need?" Vicente inquired, "Maybe while we are here, we should grab some shovels and some picks?" Ellanece shook her head, "Nope…Hogs can't eat them if they're underground." Vicente shrugged, further questioning, "What about a hog call? You know, to make sure they show up!" Ellanece began to make her way for the register, further explaining, "Yea, I don't plan on being around when they show up. I'm telling ya, them thangs are dangerous.

Ellanece purchased her can of pig attractant from the same employee who had given them such a hard time at the beginning of their endeavor. As he scanned the can, he looked to the woman and to the man whom he only assumed was her much older Hispanic boyfriend, and asked, "This was the thing you couldn't wait for? You know it's illegal and unsporting to hunt at night, right?" Perturbed by the nosiness of the young employee, Ellanece tried to think of a quick excuse, "We're uh—hunting on private land."

The employee shook his head, placing the can into a thin white plastic bag, "Doesn't matter; it's still illegal." Ellanece threw her hands up yelling, "And just who the fuck do you think you are? The goddamned Game Warden?" The kid skittishly shook his head, "N-no ma'am, I was just informing you is all." The employee finished ringing up her total, Ellanece swiped her credit card, while simultaneously flipping the young man the bird, and stated, "Inform this, Jr."

As the two got back into the vehicle, Vicente scratched his chin, stating, "You know, for a pretty young *Anglo* woman, you certainly are awfully sour in your temperament. Why is this so?" Ellanece gritted her teeth, "You know *esé*, when I woke up this morning I really wasn't expecting to have another body dropped in my home/work place…let alone have to cover up that said body—"

"—Sorry to interrupt, but again, never really heard of any white breezies being concerned with body counts." Ellanece's face lit up with an impish grin, as she leaned forward, whispering, "I ain't your average breezy—*esé!"* Ellanece started the car, placing it into drive and as they began towards the National Forrest, Vicente cleared his throat, and informed, "You are aware, that when a gringo/gringa uses the term esé to a Latino; it's the same as a white person saying nigger to a black person."

Ellanece chuckled, "Why the fuck do you think I chose to use it—esé?" Vicente's brow furrowed as he muttered under his breath, "Eres un puto picapleitos, perra!" to which Ellanece promptly responded, "Don't forget, I speak Spanish, asshole!"

It took them almost thirty minutes just to hit the entrance of the National Forrest, once the Firebird turned onto the dirt road, Vicente asked, "Forgive me for asking, but how extensive is your knowledge of these woods?" Grimacing, she replied, "little to none." Vicente twitched his nose and replied, "So how exactly do you plan on finding any hogs?"

Pounding her fist on the steering wheel she shouted angrily, "Shit man, I dunno? Only plan I really got is this: Drive as deep out into these woods as this car will permit, unload the body and detonate the goddamn hog bomb. Because, that's what the motherfucker is for, attracting hogs."

"¡Jesús Cristo! Have you ever even been hunting before?" With a wry look upon her face she retorted, "Sort of." Her response only baffled Vicente, "*Sort of*? How the hell does one sort of go hunting?" Rolling her eyes, she replied, "You know, like videogames and junk."

Giving a violent shrug, he exclaimed, "¡Dios mío! Tienes que estar bromeando, perra." Ellanece cackled to his response, "I'm a fucking millennial, the hell did you expect?" After several miles of driving and the dirt path they had been driving down, had turned into a little more than a cut out trail, Ellanece placed her car into park, stating, "Alright, this spot's as good as any." Once Ellanece killed the engine, Vicente inquired, "I know it may be a little late for this—but what if there aren't any hogs in these woods?" What will you do if the body is found?"

"I'm not the one that killed the guy, so it's not really my problem." Vicente locked his door and crossed his arms replying, "You're lack of knowledge and concern, have me not wanting to go through with this plan."

"For fuck's sake, you're an illegal! Once we are done here, if you're that paranoid, then skip on over a few counties, you'll be alright." Vicente shook his head, "Nope, if it were to ever lead back to you, I do not think I can trust you, gringa." Not only was she growing impatient, but she was also growing angry, with Vicente's new found insubordination. "Fine, asshole, you're not gonna get any extra money for helping me dispose of the body."

Tilting his head, with an askew frown, he retorted, "That suck's. But I would rather have it that way, then worry with any potential loose ends with you." It was at this time, that Ellanece reached down into her purse, retrieving her pink polymered .380, "You wanna talk about *loose ends* get the hell out of my car, esé!" Not expecting the petit American woman to produce a loaded gun, he panicked, scrambling to make his way out of the car, once he was actually able to get the car door open, he tumbled backwards out of the door.

Scramble for the woods. He thought to himself. Unfortunately for him, though, Ellanece, had also been quick to flawlessly make her way out of the car, screaming, "Freeze" cracking off a shot, as soon as he made it to his feet.

Making like a statue, he calmly enlightened, "You kill me, and you'll just have to dead Mexicans on your hands." Pulling the release for the back hatch, she commanded, "Yea well, get that body out the back of my car, and we'll talk options." Vicente slowly made his way to the back of the vehicle, making it a point not to make any eye contact with gun wielding maiden. He lifted the hatch, and hoisted the body out of the car. "Don't just lay the bastard there, behind my car, drag his ass off to the side there."

Vicente shook his head, "Not till we talk options—I gotta know I'm gonna walk away from this whole situation."

"Well fine…tell me what you want me to do, so that you'll stop whining like a little bitch, and move that goddamn body." Wiping the sweat from his brow, he began to list off his commands, "For starters, you can put that piece away, then, you can give me the rest of the money you owe me, and lastly, we're in this shit together, gringa, you want this body moved so bad? You're gonna have to come over here and help me move it!"

Knowing that Vicente outweighed and muscled her, she knew getting anywhere close to him would put her at a high risk: *Fuck it*. She thought to herself: *Bang!* She fired a shot, hitting Vicente over the top right cheek bone, his hands flying up to cover the wound, his torso contorting as he dropped to the floor beside Gustavo.

Keeping the gun ready to fire at a moment's notice, she slowly crept her way around the tail of her Firebird. Looking over her hatch, all she could see was Vicente's body violently convulsing, as his arms drew up tight to his chest. Once Vicente stopped convulsing and had finally passed away, Ellanece, retrieved the Hog bomb from the trunk of her car and slammed the hatch shut.

Before she engaged the bomb, she stripped both men of their clothing, making sure she retrieved all of the cash which she had paid Vicente. However, upon further inspection of his wallet, Ellanece came across a major problem, Vicente, had a green card, "Fuck me!" She muttered to herself, realizing, that instead of having two dead illegals that would never be missed or cared for by authorities, she had one legal that after a certain amount of time would definitely become of concern to local Law Enforcement.

Using the flashlight app on her phone, she looked around for the dispensed shells from her gun, knowing the shells had full and partial prints on them. After finding the last shell, she tossed them inside of her vehicle, then the thought crossed her mind: *If he's gotta green-card, there's probably a chance he's got dental records, body ever gets found, it won't matter how much of him, the pigs eat.*

Reaching into her vehicle, she once again popped the hatch. Making her way back to the rear of her car, she dug through the trunk till she produced a tire iron. She then bent down over Vicente's body, squared his jaw up, with the tire iron, and continued to unmercifully pound he end of the tire iron across the dead man's teeth till they were all knocked out of his head.

Standing up, covered in blood spatter, all she could do was ignite the hog bomb and pray that pig's would come by and gnaw the man's finger prints from his body along with anything else that may identify the man to authorities. She placed the bomb directly between the two men, the ripped the tab causing a thick orange cloud of sow estrus and hog urine.

The stench almost made her vomit as she raced to the driver side seat, slamming the door shut. She started engine, threw the car into reverse and backed over the bodies and hog bomb. The gaseous orange smoke covering the vehicle, infiltrating the inside through the AC vents. As the car rolled over the two bodies, the weight of the vehicle crushed the rib cages of the men, leaving tire imprints on their soon to be rotting flesh.

By the time she arrived home the hours had crept into the wee hours of the morning. Entering in through the back door of her house, she was not only covered in blood but was also stained orange from the hog-bomb. The first thing she did was grab a Hefty Bag out from under the kitchen sink. She then made her way back to her car and collected the dead men's belongings, then while still being under the cover of darkness she stripped out of the clothes that she was wearing and placed them in the bag too.

Trotting in the nude, over to her water spigot, she turned on the water valve, and picked the green and yellow hose up to wash as much blood, feral hog estrus, and pig urine off of her. After getting the majority of the mess off her she made her way into her house and up into her upstairs bathroom, where she finished cleaning herself up. Upon getting out of the shower, she kept in mind, that not only the outside, but the inside of her car, were still covered in an orange film of the hog-bomb. So in choosing her next pair of clothes, she made it a point to pick garments that she wouldn't mind having to dispose of if she couldn't get the stench from the film out.

Finally making it back out to her car, where she had everything linking her to the crime, wrapped up in huge black Hefty-Bag; she took notice of the time: *3:30 am.* The sun would be rising soon, and she needed a place to dispose the evidence. Burning it was the first and most permanent solution, unfortunately though, not only was her county under a strict no burn ordinance, but it was also too close to dawn for sleeping neighbors to not notice.

Another option would be dumping it in the Archusa Creek Lake, or the Chickasawhay River, but for that she would need access to a boat; something she did not have. So she figured that if she couldn't dump or burn the evidence she was going to have to bury it in plain sight. Tapping her finger to her chin, she thought to herself: *The wall to the master bedroom still needs work done to it!*

She gathered the bag, and hauled the proof of her crime right up the stairs, on the way up, she grabbed a crowbar; and upon entering the bedroom, she dropped the bag and began swinging at the wall, demolishing chunks of drywall with every blow, till finally she had a hole big enough to stuff the evidence down in between the walls. All she had left to do was to wait till the local hardware store opened, and purchase the supplies necessary to cover up the hole in the wall.

Chapter V

The Detectives of Bucksdale

Being a detective in the south is sometimes one of the hardest places on earth, for a detective to do good *police-work*. It can be really tricky trying to decipher who is guilty when you live in a community where even the criminals are polite and have good manners. Take Ellanece for example, a drop dead gorgeous Bama-Bombshell, who also just so happened to have a little bit of a murderous streak in her. Though Detective Lewis had pretty much cleared Ellanece on the Henderson Murder Case, there was still the matter of having her cleared in a court of law.

Detective Lewis was a quiet man and he liked the fact that he lived in a quiet town. Bucksdale being the small town that it was, meant that it also had a really small police force, seeing as how it rarely saw anything big and exciting, like cops in the big city would.

Aside from the Chief, the BPD was headed by Captain Walter Burton. He was a large gray headed man, in his mid-sixties and had almost forty years of experience in law enforcement, twenty years earlier he had served as a detective just like Lewis. Next in command was Lieutenant Edward Pogue, who was in his late forties, but was often mistaken for being in his late thirties, due to his built physique, thick hairline and overall lack of wrinkles in his face.

Then there's Detective Jasper Lewis, a Sergeant, who was in his mid-thirties; and under Lewis was Detective Traci Harmon, a rough looking blonde in her early thirties, who rarely wore any makeup, and could hold her own with even some of the toughest of men. Because she was new to the detective unit, and had very little say so in how things were ran. However, she did hold the privilege of being the first female detective for the BPD; and also, held the unfortunate position of being the partner of Detective Jasper Lewis.

Other than Detective Harmon and the three other commissioned officers; the BPD was comprised of six uniformed officers, which allowed for two uniformed Officers for each shift, Sara Mathews and Michael Hicks in the morning. During the evening, Officers Patrick Griffin and Spencer Jones; and on the grave yard shift was Officers Earl Roberts and Donald Wayne.

In the following days after Lewis had opened the Henderson Case; Lewis was sitting in his office, filling out paper work, for the courts; when all of a sudden he was interrupted by a loud knock. Lewis looked up from his desk, and saw Lieutenant Pogue who was leaning half way into the office, supporting himself on the door frame, with a wide smile on his face.

"May I help you, sir?" Lewis asked in a sarcastic tone. The Lieutenant responded with a similar attitude, "You sure can my man, starting by getting off your ass, and following me down to the Captain's office, he's called us in for a meeting." Tossing his pen down onto his desk and leaning back in his chair, rubbing his hands over his face, Lewis groaned, "Oh, all right... if you say so." Lewis reluctantly got up from his chair and followed the Lieutenant down the hall to the Captain's office.

As Detective Lewis entered the office, he was surprised to see Detective Harmon sitting in a chair, waiting on him and the Lieutenant to arrive. Pogue gently shut the door behind them, and the two men found their seats beside Harmon.

The Captain cleared his throat and a said, "Gentlemen, so glad y'all could join us on this fine morning. Now, before I go any further, if I told ya that I was the one calling this meeting, I'd be lying to you. With that being said, Detective Harmon, the floor is all yours." Harmon, who was sitting in between Lewis and Pogue, silently arose from her seat; as she did so, Lewis slid his right foot all the way out if front of him, and twisted his torso, so that he was more or less facing her.

Harmon looked to all three of the men before speaking, then, taking in a deep breath, she said, "Chief, I have called this meeting before you all today, because, I feel that it was wrong for Sergeant Lewis to be the sole Detective, to work the Henderson Murder Case. Also, I can't help but feel that I was left out, not only because of my lack of experience, but also, due to the fact that—"

"—Oh, for *fuck's* sake," Lewis interrupted, "if you say I left you out of the murder case because you're a woman, you got another thing coming to ya." Harmon turned to Lewis, now focusing all of her attention on him. "Excuse me, Sergeant Lewis, but your lead suspect was in fact a *female*; who's only lived here for six months mind you; and the murdered victim, was a lifelong resident of the town."

Lewis, doing his best to hide his anger, quickly stood up, looked to Harmon, and said, "Have a seat *Detective* Harmon, while I unnecessarily explain my actions." Lewis kept his eyes locked onto Harmon, until she was completely seated, he then continued, "Captain, as you know, on the night that Dennis Henderson was slain; I was the Detective *on call*. Now, should I have called my partner, Detective Harmon, in on the case, maybe so? But seeing as how murder is a rare occurrence here in town, I wasn't sure of how dangerous the circumstances might be."

Harmon quickly commented, "All the more reason that Detective Lewis should have called me in for back up!" Lewis held up his index finger, saying, "Sir, there was absolutely no need for me to request for Detective Harmon's back up, in regards to my safety. When I arrived the grave shift had a perimeter locked down and everything."

Harmon was quick to reply, "I'm not trying to undermine anybody here; I just feel that as an investigation unit, we could have handled the case better. I mean, after all, Ellanece Mosley has only been interrogated here at the station, *once*, and by *one* Detective, we didn't even get a chance to play *good-cop bad-cop*."

"Is that why you became a Detective, Harmon? So you could play a TV drama cop?" Lewis added. The more Harmon picked at reasons for why Lewis should have included her on the case, the more aggravated he became. "Sir there is a reason why I'm closing this case as soon as I am. Just as there is also a reason, as to why Ms. Mosley was only interrogated here the one time."

Lewis paused, taking a moment to look at Harmon, then to the Lieutenant, and finally back to the Captain. "When I first brought, Ms. Mosley in for questioning, I wanted to believe, more than anything, that she was the perp. However, throughout my investigation, overwhelming evidence, from Mr. Henderson's past, pointed out that he had a history of sexual misconduct. I had not only his mother; but also had his SAA counselor, and e-mail history on his laptop to confirm that he was more than capable of trying to rape someone; and looking at all of the Craigslist adds that he had responded to… he seemed mighty desperate to get laid."

"Is there any evidence that Mosley invited Henderson over to her house for any sexual favors?" asked Harmon.

"Yes, Ms. Mosley even admitted in her statement, that she had consumed a few alcoholic beverages, invited Henderson to her home, then changed her mind upon his arrival."

It was now Lieutenant Pogue who came to stand up and speak, "Sir, just really quick, I would just like to add, that I was fully aware of the situation at hand and allowed, Detective Lewis to handle this case on his own." The Captain causally leaned forward, clasping his hands together, allowing them to rest on his desk, he cleared his throat and adjusted his glasses and said, "Well with everything that has been presented here before me today, I really don't see what the problem is Detective Harmon. If Lieutenant Pogue, saw fit for Sergeant Lewis to handle a murder case on his own, then that's the Lieutenant's decision, and I trust his judgment completely."

The room fell awkwardly silent, The Captain looked around to everyone, waiting on any follow-up statements, after realizing that no one was going to speak up he concluded, "Well that seems to clear everything up. I'm glad we were able to resolve this in such a timely fashion. Detective's, keep up the good work, y'all are dismissed."

The Captain's office doors flung open and Harmon and Lewis exited, meanwhile the Lieutenant and the Captain stayed behind. As the two Detectives, hastily walked down the precinct corridors, Lewis looked over to Harmon and demanded in sharp tone, "Detective Harmon, my office, *now*!" Harmon rolled her eyes and followed Lewis into his office.

As the two detectives entered, Lewis slammed the door as hard as he could behind them. Harmon plopped down, in front of Lewis's desk, while Lewis fiercely circled around behind it, and exclaimed, "Just who the hell do you think you are?" Lewis paused, trying to keep his composure, "You realize that you just went above your *boss's boss* with a complaint, right? Also, might I add, that was totally *unprofessional* of you!" Harmon innocently raised her hand, and Lewis snapped at her, "Oh for Christ sake, don't patronize me, if ya got something to say, then say it."

"Well sir, my only concern was that Ms. Mosley might have beguiled you to form a biased decision."

"No ma'am, don't you even try to go down that road! I've never met a single person in my life that I let get in the way of me doing my job right! And I ain't about to let some outta town tramp start now, are we perfectly clear on that?" Harmon nodded and added, "Yes sir, I wasn't trying to implicate you in anything, I was simply trying to suggest, that a second opinion always helps."

Lewis got up from where he was seated, grabbed a hold of his belt buckle, and silently walked around his desk, to the chair, which Harmon was sitting in. He placed his hands on the arm rest of her chair and leaned in and said, "I ain't trying to implicate you in anything either, I'm simply suggesting that if you don't stop trying to keep this case I'm closing, open; I'll have no choice but to tell everyone how Ms. Mosley outbid you on that house, and that that's the real reason why I left you off the case."

Harmon was surprised that Lewis had known about her attempt to bid on the Victorian six months ago, and also knew that he had just put her in checkmate. She nodded her head, and in almost a whisper of a voice said, "Yes sir." Lewis nodded back and pulled away from her, leaning back on his desk, folding his arms across his chest and turning his head to the side to look out of his window. "Besides, to me it looks a lot better, having the

Sergeant looking out for his rookie detective; rather than us turning this entire department into an internal affairs wet dream.

"You realize if we found that bitch guilty and you had helped in the investigation, her lawyers would have had a field day." Harmon once again nodded quietly, Lewis then added, "Alright, you're dismissed." Harmon was quick to shoot up out of her seat, she had just made her way to the door, placing her hand on the knob when Lewis said, "Oh and Detective Harmon," she stopped and slowly twisted her head to look back at her Sergeant, "you ever go over my head like this again, and I will personally see to it, that you spend the rest of your career at the end of the local high school lunch line." Harmon nodded and quickly continued to make her way out of his office.

Chapter VI

A Morbid Trend for Church Street

The next five months in Bucksdale were fairly quiet, Ellanece was cleared in a court of law, and found justified in the killing of Denis Henderson. Not that the case hadn't raised any eyebrows amongst the locals, unfortunately though for the late Mr. Henderson and his mother, his history of sexual deviancy had him done in from the very beginning.

Other than that, the town of Bucksdale had remained the slow-paced, quiet community, which Detective Lewis loved so much. However, on the afternoon of Friday, October 8th, Jasper Lewis found himself standing in front of a staircase landing, staring down at a stiff, at the residence of none other than 300 East Church Street. Only on this occasion, he hadn't come alone. This time he arrived along with Detective Traci Harmon.

The two Detectives, along with Ellanece, the County Coroner, and the recently deceased's apprentice, all stood gathered around the fresh corpse. Ellanece was wearing a white dress, accented with black buttons in the middle, which ran down all the way to the center until they met a black belt, which stylishly wrapped all the way around her petite waist. The dress part, was embroidered with black lace flowers. She stood with her hands posted on her hips, elbows pointing out in opposite directions.

Harmon was quick to notice that her attire was a little bit more on the fancy side of casual, "I don't know how this could have happened," Ellanece stated, "he must have tripped or lost his balance, or something, because, he was alone when he had gone upstairs." The female detective made her way over to Ellanece, and asked, "Why had he gone upstairs alone? And is there anyone who can confirm that he was alone when he decided to come down the stairs?"

The young assistant was more than eager to raise his hand and without even being given permission to talk, he said, "Yea, I can! I was outside and had just begun painting the side front wall, when I heard him shuffle up the stairs, I even peered in through the window, and saw him waddling up them. Ella was in the kitchen. Being fairly hot for an October day, I quickly found myself parched, and dehydrated; so I and had gone into the kitchen to grab a drink of water. It was there in the kitchen that Ella and I both heard him tumble down the staircase."

As the young man finished, Harmon took note of his attire as well. Clean khaki pants, with work boots and a white t-shirt with fresh paint on it. "You always paint in your khaki's, son?" The young man smiled and replied, "Oh no ma'am, these ain't khaki's; they're Carhartts."

"They certainly do appear to be very clean, compared to your t-shirt and boots."

"I usually have a painter's smock on, it gets too hot, to have hanging all the way around my neck, so I usually just wrap it around my waist." Harmon began to jot notes down; using her iPhone, "How old are you, son?" asked Lewis, now also taking an interest in the young man.

The young man replied, "I'm nineteen. Also, if it's all the same to you Detective, I'm a grown man, and I prefer to be referenced as Sir or Mr." Lewis nodded and said, "Of course you do, my apologies. So what's your name, *Mister*?" Harmon was still fixated on the young man, and she watched as he suspiciously glanced from Detective Lewis, over to Ellanece.

Harmon's eyes now shifting over to Ellanece, she witnessed as the woman surreptitiously nodded her head, before the man answered, "Name's Justin Howard, I'm Mr. Clarke's personal assistant/protégé." Not wanting Mr. Howard to receive any more coaching advice from Ellanece, Harmon interjected "Alright, I think now's a good time that Detective Lewis and I take the two of you, into separate rooms, for questioning."

Not liking that his rookie Detective, had just given a deliberate command, without even trying to consult him first, Lewis called out for the two uniforms working the perimeter to stand and watch the two witnesses/possible suspects. Lewis placed an arm around Harmon and guided her into one of the other rooms, once in private he hissed, "What the *hell* do you think you are doing? This is my investigation; I call the shots!" Harmon motioned for Lewis to bring his head closer, so that she could whisper into his ear, "Sir, you didn't see what I saw." Leaning back so that he could make eye contact with her, he seethed, "You'd better not be talking about the nod."

Harmon's eyes widened and her jaw dropped, "You saw the nod, why didn't you do anything? She was obviously instructing him." Lewis replied in an aggravated tone, "Yea, maybe so. Or maybe she just happened to have a muscle spasm, right before he answered. But now—*thanks to you* and your impatience, I won't be able to ask any more questions with them both in the same room to find out."

Realizing the mistake, she had just made, she shook her head, cursing herself and said, "Shit—my bad, I should've known better."

"Damn right, you should've! More importantly, you should remember who the hell is in charge; and to not go bossing people around on the fly like that." She quietly bowed her head, and Lewis continued, "Well, no use frettin' about it, what's done is done. You take Ellanece and I'll take the Howard kid." Surprised at what he had just said, she replied, "You mean you're actually gonna give me a lick at Ellanece?" Lewis cracked a smile and answered, "Yea, I figured you been itching long enough to talk to her, plus, I think I can work a *buddy angle* on the kid." Harmon smiled and nodded and the two detectives exited the room.

As they entered back into the living room where everyone was standing, Lewis grabbed Justin by the arm and said, "Come with me—*mister.*" Harmon approached Ellanece, asking if there was another room in the house that she would feel more comfortable talking in. She wanted Ellanece to feel like she was more interested in helping her out, rather than feeling like she was being interrogated. Ellanece nodded, and said, "The other end of the house is fine."

"Good," Lewis stated, "Mr. Howard and I will take the sun-room." Lewis nudged Howard with his forearm and the two began to walk. Harmon, taking a gentler approach, asked for Ellanece to lead the way.

Lewis and Justin entered the sun room, Lewis posted up against one of the windows, bringing his right foot up, to rest on the wall. Howard paced a small span of three to four steps, back and forth nervously, and the detective began his barrage of questioning, "So, you're a young guy, how'd ya come to work as a painters assistant?" Justin stopped pacing, just long enough to give an answer, folding his arms in front of him, "Mr. Clarke's office, was right down the street from where my dad works. I've known of him ever since I was like, twelve. Anyway, I didn't get to work with him till I was seventeen.

"My parents were in the middle of remodeling our home. Not wanting to screw the walls up by painting 'em themselves; they hired Mr. Clarke's company, to come paint for them. The whole time they was there painting; I was home, on summer vacation. I didn't have a job, so I was home alone, while they worked. Well, one day, out of boredom; I asked if there was anything I could do to help. Long story short, I wound up not only having a blast but also turned out I had a knack for Painting. Anyway, as soon as I graduated high school, Mr. Clarke, hired me on as his full time assistant."

Lewis nodded and typed a note down in his iPhone, and y'all are from this county, or what?" Justin was quick to answer, "No sir, we're from Hinds County, based outta Jackson." Lewis nodded once again, "My, that's one hell of a daily commute, damn near three counties, ain't it?"

"More like two and a half. Also, there is no daily commute; I've been living here in Bucksdale for the last four and a half months."

"Where, have you been shacking up at, the Minx-Winx?" Lewis asked.

"Yea, at first I was staying at the *Minx-Winx-Inn*; but Ella and I seemed to hit it off pretty well, and she told me not to tell Mr. Clarke that I was staying here with her. That he might get upset if he found out we was living together while I was working on the clock for him."

Lewis found it odd that such a young man was on a first-name basis, with his employer's client, who was almost ten years his senior. It was then that he noticed a light pink smudge across Justin's upper lip; it was light in color and from across the room could maybe be mistaken as the beginnings of a cold sore.

Just to be sure, he took his hand placing the tips of his fingers on the kid's cheek and swiping his thumb across Justin's mouth. "What the fuck man?" Justin exclaimed pushing the Detective away from him. Lewis ignored him, investigating the residue which was now on his thumb. He rubbed his thumb and index finger together; he then brought his thumb up to his mouth and touched it with the tip of his tongue.

He took a moment to savor the sweet flavor. Then continued, "Ya know, I could swear one of my ex-girlfriends had the exact same lipstick. Question is, if I go across this house and give Ms. Mosley a big wet kiss on the mouth, am I gonna taste the same thing I just tasted on my thumb?" Justin's brow furrowed and he fired back, "Dude. Are you insane? I can't be mixing business and pleasure; that's the whole reason Ella didn't want me telling Mr. Clarke I was living here, she was afraid that he would get the wrong idea, besides, the lipstick is from my girlfriend from back home, she stopped in town for a few hours and we made out." Lewis had his eyes squinted, squeezing them tight, at how naïve the young man was. "You really think I'm that stupid kid?"

Justin was quick to look up and said, "I thought we had an understanding on how I wanted to be addressed?" Lewis drew his right hand back and open-handedly smacked Justin across the side of the head, "Then start answering my questions like a fuckin' grown-ass man, and quit lying to me, as if you're some scared little boy. You've already admitted that you and Ms. Mosley hit it off very early in your stay, and that she offered to lodge you for free.

"Also, in the short time I have been here today, I have heard you call her on a first name basis several times; and now as I am questioning you; I find the same shade of lipstick that she was wearing on your mouth!"

"*Okay!*" Justin shouted, "But you just have to promise, that you won't tell her I told you." Trying to regain the young man's trust, Lewis shrugged his shoulders, and stuck a closed hand out for a fist bump and said, "*Bro-code*, dude." Justin let out a sigh of relief, and as he bumped fists with the Detective he said with a cocksure grin, "Yea, I've been tapping that. 'bout the last two months; I been sleeping in her room almost every night."

Lewis's mouth took the shape of an upside down U and he nodded his head up and down, "So what's in it for you?" Lewis asked. A dumbfounded look appeared on Justin's face and he exclaimed with a shrug, "Uh—*Pussy*! Duh dude." Lewis broke out into a brief fit of laughter. "What's so fucking funny?" Justin asked in an angered tone. Lewis stuck his hand out and said, "My bad, I do apologize. It's just—that's the best response, any nineteen-year-old, could've ever given me!" Now, more confused than ever Justin asked, "I don't get it."

"Sir, you mean to tell me that you been shacking up here, and bedding Ms. Mosley for free?" Justin thought about the question, and then answered, "Yea, I guess you could say that, why?" Lewis placed a hand on the young man's shoulder, "Let me throw ya a tip, Mr. Howard; one that only *real men* come to usually find out the hard way. When it comes to *sex*, if it ain't coming from your wife or longtime girlfriend—*sex ain't ever free*. Whether you pay out of wallet, or with a piece of your soul, you're gonna wind up paying for it somehow."

Lewis paused and let his advice set in. "Anyway, I think you've told me all I need to know for now." As the Detective turned to go back inside the house, Justin grabbed his arm, and asked out of desperation, "You still promise not to tell Ella, right?" Lewis nudged him on the shoulder and with a cheesy smile replied, "Bro-code man, *it's sacred*."

After the two detectives were done with their questioning, they met in the kitchen and had the uniformed officers sit with the now confirmed suspects, in two separate parts of the house, to keep

Ellanece and Justin from conspiring any further. Quickly deciding that before they share any notes they should see everything the Coroner had found; they met up with the Coroner back at the staircase where, the corpse still laid out. "Mr. Powell," said Lewis, "I hope you found something that can maybe give us a break in the Clarke case." Powell nodded and replied, "When I first began to examine the body, I thought that maybe he had actually slipped and fallen on his own—"

"—But," Lewis interrupted, Mr. Powell shot him an annoyed look and continued, "—I began my examination, at the top of the head where he sustained a contusion, to the left corner of his for head, it looked innocent enough, at first, till I noticed that he had a blown pupil in his left eye.

"This caused me to reexamine the contusion, and after taking some measurements I've concluded, that the wound was deeper, than if he had sustained it from just an innocent fall. As I made my way further down his face I noticed that the man's left cheek had come into contact with that of another hand, most likely a slap, if I am reading the red patch correctly.

"Upon further inspection I noticed by the positioning of the head, that his neck had been broken, I checked for any hand or ligature marks, and found none. So I am assuming that if the man did fall, he landed on his head, snapping his neck. If he indeed fell down the stairs then he died at the very top, because there should have been a lot more bruising to go along with all of the injuries that he sustained.

"Lastly, and I almost over looked this, but as I got to the man's ankles, which I only decided to check, to see if he had any marks or bruising, to indicate if he had been dangled or not. I found a semicircular bruise, around the right ankle of the man's leg. This tells me, that it's not only an intentional blow, but that it was most likely done with a cane or umbrella handle—Detectives, this man was most definitely murdered."

Walking over to have a closer look at the victim, Lewis asked, "and you're sure this red patch, came from a slap? There is no way that he could have sustained this from the tumble down the stairs?" While Lewis examined the condition of the deceased's clothes, Mr. Powell replied, "No it was most definitely a slap, a fall would have left a larger patch and darker coloring, on his face."

"Is there any way to tell if this was done by a male or female?" Harmon asked,

"Nothing that would hold up in court, but if you wanted my honest opinion; I would say that a female delivered the blow. I say this only because *men* are more prone to punching when infuriated, while *women* are more inclined to slap." Harmon bent down beside Lewis and said, "I'm seeing that the two of them got into it, while they were upstairs, Mosley slapped Clarke, for whatever reason; Clarke being a gentleman and not wanting to strike a lady, furiously turned around to go down the stairs—"

"—Mosley not being through," Lewis interrupted, "walked up behind Clarke, grabbed a cane—or something similar, and whacked his foot out from under him, causing him to fall to his death."

Raising a finger, the Coroner added, "Keep in mind though, that there is the possibility that Clarke could have been caught staring at her, ahem—*goods*, as he entered through the front door, warranting a slap from Ms. Mosley. I'm only telling you what a good defense attorney would say in the court room."

"What about the time of death, do you know that one yet?" Lewis asked.

Powell replied, "Yea, I haven't taken his liver temp, I'll know more once I've done that, so far though, judging from the waxy appearance of the man's skin, the bluing around the lips, and whitening around the nails he was killed at least thirty minutes ago. That being said, there's no blanching of the skin, when being touched, so it's at least less than three hours old." Harmon shot a look to Lewis and asked, "Do you recall what this was called in as?" Lewis nodded and replied, "Yea, they called it in as an accident, and EMT's called us in after they discovered that he was dead."

Lewis and Harmon thanked Mr. Powell and then broke off to compare notes with one another. Lewis asked first, "So what all did you get from Ellanece?"

"Nothing really, just that they were both down-stairs when Clarke fell; which we both now know to be a load of bull shit."

"Did she say anything about the kid shacking up with her?"

A surprised look dawned upon Harmon's face, eyes wide open, eyebrows raised to form perfect arches as her jaw once again unhinged leaving her mouth ajar, and she exclaimed, *"No!"* Lewis's lips tightened and he blinked twice as he turned his head to the side, "Alright," he said, "I've just about had enough, one of those two, killed that man, and neither one of them are coming forward about it; not to mention the fact that all the evidence I've seen here today, points to our girl, Ellanece, being the perp. Get Mosley and the kid into the back of a patrol car, so that we can bring 'em down to the station for questioning. I'm gonna tell CSI to look and collect every cane and umbrella that's in this house.

Back at the station, Ellanece sat in one interrogation room, while Justin sat in the other. Ellanece sat calm, cool, and collected. Her hands neatly folded on the table, waiting for one of the Detectives to enter. Justin, on the other hand, was a nervous wreck. In each room instead of a big two-way mirror, there was in its place one camera pointed at the table where the suspects would be sitting.

Lewis and Harmon watched from the computer in his office, how each suspect was reacting to being in an interrogation room. "Look at how calm she is." Harmon said. Lewis replied, "Eerie ain't it. She was just about the same way with me when I brought her in for questioning a couple of months ago."

"On the other hand, the kid looks like he's about to have a heart attack. I've never seen anyone pace so frantically."

"What we have here, is the contrast between an interrogation room *veteran* and *virgin*. Ellanece is far too versed when it comes to questioning. Let's swap it up, you take the boy and I'll take Ellanece, they probably won't be expecting it, at the very least, I know the kid won't. Be supportive with him, and only push him if you have too. I Think we can get him to turn on Ellanece if we play our cards right." Harmon nodded and the two detectives split to go interrogate their suspects.

Detective Lewis entered the room where Ellanece was patiently waiting. As he closed the door behind him, and she saw who it was, she broke a smile and greeted him with a warm greeting, "Detective, I was wondering when I was gonna get some one-on-one time with you again."

Lewis casually sat down across the table from her and said, "Ms. Mosley, if *one-on-one time* is what you want with me, then you've gotta to find a better way than having dead men turn up inside your home." Ellanece's lips tightened as she straightened up in her seat, she stuck her tits out, in a cheap attempt to try and seduce the detective into falling soft, and taking it easy on her, she cleared her throat and said, "I haven't kilt nobody, detective."

"Cut the cute country talk Mosley. It may work on some guys, but it's not gonna work on me, I know you're educated, and I know you speak proper English, so use it." Ellanece rolled her eyes and replied, "Nothing gets past you does it Detective."

"Nope sure doesn't, it's kind of what they pay me to do. On that note, ya mind telling me how long you've been bedding the boy and why?" A sincere look of surprise painted her face and she quickly tried to cover it, but it was too late, Lewis had already seen that he had shaken her. "What gave it away?"

Lewis leaned back in his chair and thought for a moment. "You know what?" he said, "I'm gonna be honest with you, and instead of saying that he was quick to brag about how he was screwing an older woman. It was in fact, a lipstick smear on his upper lip. He tried to say it was the doing of a *girlfriend*." Ellanece twisted her lips, thinking and finally batted back with, "Okay fine, you got me. I've been sleeping with him. But it's nobody's business with whom I share my bed with, as long as it's with another consenting adult; and believe me Detective, he was more than just consenting!"

Lewis responded with a chuckle and said, "Oh I bet he was! I remember being nineteen, beer and sex were about all I could keep my mind focused on. Thank the Lord I eventually grew out of all that and decided to do something useful with my life. And you are right, as long as the other partner is a consenting adult—whom you fool around with, is none of my business. Except, there seems to be some pattern forming between: *you, sex, and dead guys*."

Back in the second Interrogation room where, Justin was frantically pacing, he was interrupted, when he heard a knock come from the door, and Detective Harmon, entered the room. "Mr. Howard, how's it going, and please, take a seat. So I can begin questioning, I'm required by law to ask you if you would like an attorney to be present with you at this time." The two became seated at opposite ends of the table, and almost as soon as Justin's butt hit the seat of his chair, his right knee frantically started to pop up and down. "Am I under arrest?" Harmon shook her head, and replied, "Under arrest, for what?"

"You know—my dead boss."

"Are you the one who killed your boss?" she asked coolly. "No, I didn't kill him; no one did… he fell." Harmon bore a half crooked smile and replied, "Then no, you are not under arrest at this time, you are simply a suspect, being detained and interrogated, about the untimely death of one Farrington Clarke. My first real question being: Are you sure you don't want your attorney present?" Justin took in a deep breath and replied, "No, I'm good."

"So how long have you and Ms. Mosley been an *item* with one another?" Justin bolted up out of his chair in anger sending his chair falling over backwards, and yelled, "He promised he wouldn't fucking tell!" Harmon leaned back and threw a hand out to try and calm him down, "Whoa there, partner, just hold up. He promised that he wouldn't tell *Ellanece* because he used the *bro-code* on you. He never said anything about not telling me, and since I lack certain parts in my nether regions, to allow me to join the ranks of the *bro's* there is absolutely nothing stopping me from telling Ellanece, that you told Detective Lewis, that the two of you have been sleeping together."

Justin cursed under his breath. "Yea," followed Harmon, "he out smarted ya, didn't he? With that being said, let me let you in on something. Everyone in this unfortunate situation, except for you, is over the age of twenty-five. And everyone in this situation is more than capable of outsmarting you, and using you for their best interest.

"Now, you very well may be an adult, but you are still a very young adult, and you still got your training wheels on. Now I am more than willing to be your guide, and me being your guide, puts me in your corner, and I promise you that I won't steer you down the wrong path. Now—how about you pick your chair up and calmly sit back down."

Justin silently nodded once again, still being a little too scared to say anything, he slowly turned around, and picked his chair up, continuing to sit himself back down in it, as he had been instructed to do so. After becoming seated and pulling himself back up to the table, Detective Harmon returned to her questioning, "How long have you and Ms. Mosley been physical with one another?

"A couple of months or something close." He answered.

"Was there any kind of bad blood between Ms. Mosley and Mr. Clarke?"

"No, not at all."

"What about between you, and Mr. Clarke? I'm not asking, to imply that you killed him, I'm simply asking, because due to the age difference between you and Ms. Mosley, and the fact that you were regularly having intercourse, any altercation you may have had with Mr. Clarke, might have given her some weird *cougarish* instinct to protect you."

Disgusted with her allegations, Justin rolled his eyes and said, "I already told you that Ella and I were both in the kitchen when Mr. Clarke fell down the stairs." Shaking her head, she stood up and said, "You know what? It really pisses me off when someone that I am trying to help won't let me help them, because they are lying to me."

"I'm not lying."

"Yes you are, Justin! Now, as somebody that is in your corner, and interested only in *your* wellbeing, I'm going to tell you something that I normally wouldn't tell a suspect. Something that you can bet your ass Detective Lewis would *never* tell you, no matter how buddy-buddy he pretended to be with you.

"The coroner examined the corpse of Mr. Clarke, and found evidence that your boss had not only been slapped on the face before his death, but also, that there was bruising around his ankle, indicating that he was tripped. Not only that, but the blow to the head was deeper, than it normally should've been coming from an *innocent* fall. Now, that means that someone snuck up behind him and tripped him up. And seeing as how there were only three people in that house, it was either you or Ellanece."

Detective Harmon decided to let what she had said, settle with the guy. Justin who was now as white as a ghost, sat quietly for the longest time, not saying one word. At times sitting so quietly that it was hard for Harmon to even tell if he was breathing; growing impatient she added, "Look Justin, I'm going to need an answer, from you, sometime today—and I warn you, ya better be honest with me, because, one more lie out of you, and I will no longer be in your corner and you will be left out on your own."

Another moment of silence passed and much to Harmon's surprise she heard Justin say, "Okay it was me, I did it. I killed my boss, Farrington Clarke." Blown away by what she had just heard, and not wanting to believe it she asked, "You did what?"

"You heard me, I killed him."

"I'm sorry, but I'm having a hard time, believing you. Usually when someone murders another person, there is something that we detectives like to call, *motive,* and I'm just not seeing any motive with you." Justin calmly got up and slowly paced back and forth, "Sure there was! The guy lets me come over to Bucksdale for my first solo job. And more or less says that it is my project and that I should just run with it. Well that would be great; if he wasn't stopping in every couple of days, and after seeing what I've done, tells me that it's wrong; and that if Ella is ever going to sell a restored Victorian, that I have to stick with a certain look and style.

"I mean, I would always try to argue with him and say, 'The colors I chose and accent patterns I used were just more of a modern style something that people my age could really like and get into.' He would always just shoot my ideas down with the dispute that, *no one my age could afford a restored Victorian*, and that I had to keep the *demographic* of who could actually afford the place in mind."

Now even more shocked that Justin had just given her a legitimate motive, she asked. "Okay, Justin. I'm still on your side. And with that being said, I'm going to ask you if you would like your lawyer to be here with you, if you can't afford one, we'll appoint one to you." Rolling his eyes, he said in a hopeless tone, "What's the point?" gazing out in a hopeless stare, "I've already ruined my life, what's the point of dragging it out any longer."

Not knowing exactly how to handle the situation, she threw her index finger up, and told Justin to give her a moment. Harmon exited the room and walked two doors down, giving one courtesy knock and then immediately entered, where she saw Lewis all up in the face of Ellanece; yelling at her, "Give me a break woman, we know that you and Clarke had been in a physical altercation, before his fall down the stairs, not only from the redness on his cheek, but from bruising around his ankle. Confess now, and I promise this will go so much smoother for you in the long—"

"—Detective Lewis, may I have a word with you for a moment out in the hall?" Lewis was quick to lunge away from Ellanece, making his way out into the hall with Detective Harmon. As they entered the hall, the door closing behind them, Harmon brought Lewis's ear close to her mouth and she whispered. "The Howard kid just admitted to killing Farrington Clarke."

Being just as shocked as Harmon had been, to hear the news, Lewis jetted for the room where Justin was being held, and as he entered, he aggressively walked straight up to the table where Justin sat, slammed both palms onto the table, and leaned forward, getting as close as he could to Justin's face and stared him right in the eyes. He kept his position locked for a moment, then forcibly broke away saying, "*Bullshit*! Those aren't the eyes of a fuckin' killer. That boy ain't killed shit in his life."

Justin called out from behind him, "It's true, Detective, Mr. Clarke was a dick, who never let me run with my own ideas. He had just stopped by today, and the first thing he did was make his way upstairs to see how I had painted the layout of the upstairs bedrooms. I followed him up there, and as we went from room to room, he cussed at every color, technique, and pattern that I had chosen. I lost my temper, grabbed him by the shirt and back handed him.

"Embarrassed by what I had just done, I instantly apologized, and he pushed me away and began to make his way towards the stairs. Right before he got to them he told me that he was not only pulling me off of the job, but that I was also fired. I became blind with rage; and as I followed up behind him that's when I saw it—a crowbar, sitting outside the hall bathroom one of the plumbers had accidentally left behind. As I grabbed it, my original plan was to hit him across the back, but I guess instinct just kicked in, and I wound up using a downward *golf swing* catching his right ankle causing him to fall down the stairs to his death."

Lewis didn't like what he had heard. But just like Harmon, he had imperceptibly become convinced, due to Justin's compelling confession. Shaking her head and pulling out her cuff's, Harmon asked, "Would you be willing to write what you just said, down as an official statement?" Justin solemnly nodded, Harmon asked him to stand up and put his hands behind his back, and placed the cuffs on him.

"Justin Howard, you are under arrest for the murder of Farrington Clarke. You have the right to remain silent. Anything you say can and will be used against you in a court of law. You have the right to talk to a lawyer and have him present during any further questioning. If you cannot afford a lawyer, one will be appointed before any further questioning, if you wish. You can decide at any time to exercise these rights and not answer any questions or make any statements."

Lewis exited and made his way back down the hall, and slowly opened the door, to the room which held, Ellanece Mosley, and as he entered the room he said, "Justin Howard just admitted to the murder of Farrington Clarke." Ellanece slowly got up, and while keeping a blank expression, began to walk towards the door. Lewis slammed the door behind him and said "Where the hell do you think you're going? Just because he confessed, doesn't mean you're free to go. It was just you three in the house, you knew the entire time who did it, and you never said a damn thing. That's obstruction of justice right there. And I'm sure if I dig enough I can probably get you for *conspiracy*."

Ellanece shook her head, "Detective, I overheard the two of them arguing upstairs, and I knew that it was because Farrington was unhappy with something Justin had probably done. Anyway, right before I heard the commotion of Farrington falling down the stairs, I heard him yell out that he was pulling Justin from the job. I didn't tell you because, Justin and I are very close with one another and I could never live with him thinking that I sold him out, or that I threw him under some proverbial bus, just to save my own ass.

"I know how this must look two dead men turning up at my place, all within the same year. Hell, the same lifetime. But I can assure you Detective, I'm innocent. And this time you better believe I want my lawyer."

Lewis let Ellanece walk that afternoon, only because he knew that since she had lawyered-up, and Howard had already confessed; trying to keep her there was a moot point. He hadn't completely dismissed her from suspicion; he still had the gut feeling that she was up to no good and that in some way or another that she had something to do with the murder of Farrington Clarke.

Chapter VII

The Fall of Farrington Clarke Pt. I

A few weeks after the incident with the two Latino helpers, Ellanece thought it best not to try her luck hiring any more illegals for anything. So when she came to a task thwarting her from an easy completion, she just had to bite the bullet and hire professionals. She had needed to call in a professional plumbing service for some of the plumbing issues, an electrician, to help bring everything up to code, and a carpenter, to deal with some of the outside rotted areas.

Finally, after all the heavy duty stuff had been done and all that was really left was painting and decorating. Ellanece figured she had better, once again, call on a professional, someone who had a good steady technique.

By doing some research, she was given the phone number to *Clarke's American Residential Painting Service LLC*, (C.A.R.P.S) out of Jackson Mississippi. She had made up her mind that this was the company she wanted helping her. Also, the sooner they could come out and help, the better. Ellanece had found the small town of Bucksdale to be a terrible little place for newcomers, and was itching to get the place sold, so she could move.

So on a Friday afternoon, she punched in the number for the C.A.R.P.S business and scheduled an appointment, for the following week. Her appointment came faster than she thought it would, and before she knew it, one week later, she found herself in a small white room, only decorated with a single fake office plant.

She was sitting on a couch, that was most likely, an IKEA product. Across from her sat a secretary at a desk made entirely made out of particle board, Ellanece couldn't help but wonder to herself: *why wouldn't such a highly recommended Painting service, have put more time and effort into decorating the interior office.*

She saw the secretary hold a hand up to her Bluetooth, nod, and look to her and say, "Mr. Clarke will see you now." Ellanece got up from where she was sitting, and as she walked to his office door, she couldn't help but think that she might have come to the wrong place.

She entered into Mr. Clarke's office and was relieved when she saw that not only had he done a very tasteful job in decorating his own office, but also, that he had pictures of prior jobs hung all over. "Please," Farrington said, as the door closed behind her, "take a moment to look around at all the photos on the wall, before you have a seat."

Ellanece did as she was told, and as she took closer looks, she could see that each photo was actually a before and after shot, and quite frankly; the pictures spoke for themselves. She was blown away by the results that she was seeing, and couldn't help but hear one of her school teachers preaching to her about how: *One should never judge a book by its cover.*

After seeing just about all she felt that she needed to see, she made her way over to the desk and stuck her hand out to introduce herself, as the gentleman took her hand she said, "Hello there, it's a pleasure to meet you Mr. Clarke, I'm Ellanece Mosley."

Chuckling to himself he said, "I'm aware of who you are, Ms. Mosley. Let me start right off the bat, by going ahead and telling you, that I don't normally *do* jobs outside of the city of Jackson. I run a local operation, and a rather small one at that. I also, rarely do more than one job at a time, and you just happened to catch me while business has been rather um—*slow.*" Farrington paused, and Ellanece couldn't help but ask, "Well sir, if you don't normally do jobs outside of Jackson, and you already know I'm in Bucksdale, damn near two counties away; why did you agree to have a meeting with me?"

Farrington leaned back into his plush leather office chair and in an almost annoyed tone, said *"Well if you'll let me finish*; I'll tell you. You mentioned that you were in the middle of remodeling an old Victorian—it just so happens that I tend to be somewhat of a *sucker* for Victorian homes. I don't know what it is about them? I just can't help but fall in love with every one that I see.

"Also, it breaks my heart when I hear of a dilapidated one, being demolished, due to it being *forgotten* by time and the new age that we live in." Farrington took another long pause, and Ellanece interrupted once again, "—So you're saying you will help me!"

"—Again Ms. Mosley, *let me finish.*"

"Sorry."

"First I would need to see pictures, then I would need to know the square footage of the place, and lastly, do you think you could house the painter, while he stayed?" Ellanece put a hand to her chest clearing her throat, "Excuse me, Painter? I was under the impression that you would have like a team of painters?"

Farrington shot a smile, which was hard to tell if it was sincere or not, as he stated, "Normally I would, but given the circumstances that I'm the one catering to you, out of town, I can only afford the one man, and he just so happens to be one of my best. He's different than any of my other employees, I guess you could say I've sort of taken him on as my *protégé.* He's helped me on several projects; I've always trusted him with small homes to do on his own in the past. However, I think that this would be the perfect *big* project for him to take on. However, before we move on any further, I'm still going to need to see some photos?"

Ellanece perked up, pulling her iPhone out of her purse, tapping madly at the screen, to get to her home pictures folder. As she arrived to it she leaned forward, reaching over the desk, to hand the phone over to Farrington, saying, "The whole album is pretty much one big before and after...I think after flipping through, you'll really be able to see how I've brought the old girl back to life."

As he began to scroll, he shook his head, with a slight smile on his face, "Call me old-fashioned, but I miss the days of flipping through a manila folder filled with thirty-five millimeter prints." To which Ellanece clicked her tongue, replying, "Awe you can't be that way. Ya gotta embrace the age we live in now, which is the age of the internet." Farrington raised an eyebrow to the young lady, "Your age is the internet age. My age on the other hand, is the thirty-five millimeter age, with beer cans that had to be opened with church-keys instead of pop-tops."

The man continued to scroll through the pictures, taking notice of some of the new carpentry that had been done, then, as he finished scrolling he inquired, "Now from what you have told me, and from what I can see, the entire home needs to be repainted, inside and out. What is the square footage, do you know?" Ellanece scoffed, "Of course I know! I would never buy something without knowing all the details of the goddamn details!"

Farrington lowered the woman's phone, informing, "My apologies, ma'am, there's no need for language such as that. I only inquired, because, it is typical of all young people, from every generation, to sometimes jump into things head first." Retrieving her phone from Farrington, Ellanece retorted, "Mea culpa on my language, I meant no offense to you. Anyways, the place is 3,179 square ft."

Licking his upper lip, he asked, "And when was it built." Ellanece threw her hands out, taking in a deep breath, "Okay, so like, when I was first scoping the place out, a neighbor had told me that the place was built in the mid to late eighteen-hundreds! So naturally, I got really stoked in buying the place. However, at the auction, I learned that it had actually been built in 1912. It's a single family home, with two bathrooms and it sits on a 0.79-acre lot."

"Hmm, 1912 huh? That's a bit late for that style home. Most Victorians were built between 1837 and 1901. However, in the Americas the architecture was used all the way up until the early forties. The project sounds like it could take a few months for just the one man to complete. First everything that was to be painted would have to be sanded down, then primed and lastly painted. As much as I would love to do the project myself, I—I just can't spend that much amount of time away from my family, but my protégé, Mr. Howard can, seeing as how he doesn't have a family of his own yet. Do you think we can strike a deal?"

Ellanece thought for a moment, then nodded her head, and winked as she replied "Yes Mr. Clarke, I think we can make this work," Farrington replied, "Good then, we have a deal. Now, normally if you were in town, the fees wouldn't be so high, but you have to understand that I have to pay to compensate Mr. Howard for the time that he is going to be spending away from his home and life, here in Jackson, as well.

"Also, I won't be able to promise a set amount, till everything is over and done with. On the other hand, I can estimate that it will be in the neighborhood of ten thousand dollars." Ellanece placed a hand on his desk and asked, "How would you like for me to go about paying you?" Leaning back in his chair he replied, "Typically I would ask for half of the original estimate now, and you pay me the rest after your home was completed...If you need, we have financing options available" she nodded and said, "I got ya—Mr. Clarke, I need you to understand that I'm working on a budget and don't have that kind of cash to shell out up front. So yea, how about we dig into some of those financing options you just mentioned.

A couple of hours later, after hashing out the rest of the financial details; Ellanece was on her way back to Bucksdale, She and Mr. Clarke had decided that it would be too much of a hassle to get Justin to follow her over to Bucksdale on the fly, so they decided to give him the weekend to pack, and wrap up any personal matters, that he might have. The plan was that Justin would leave Jackson, sometime in the morning, and arrive in Bucksdale, around noon, where he would meet up with Ellanece at her home and the two would get him settled in.

After he arrived into Bucksdale, he pulled his 2004 Ford Ranger into the driveway located at the back of the house. As he stepped out of his truck, Ellanece was already making her way out of the back door, so that she could greet the young man. Only knowing that the painter was going to be a man younger than herself, she had made it a point to doll herself up real nice, in the event he happened to be handsome, which in this case, he just so happened to be. As they shook hands, he inquired, "I take it you're Mrs. Mosley?"

Batting her eyelashes at him, she retorted, "Please, Mrs. Mosley, was my mother. My name's Ellanece." Being young and naïve, he continued to ask, "Damn! Mr. Clark didn't say she had a daughter, you're an awfully cute thing." Both of them blushing, as he continued, "Anyway, we'll have plenty of time to get to know each other, but I gotta touch base with your mom first, so that I can get settled and everything." Ellanece rolled her eyes, "My mother's dead. I'm the one you're supposed to be *touching base* with."

Justin took a few steps back till he backed into his truck, "What?" Ellanece chuckled, holding a hand up, "Relax, it's okay. I shouldn't have greeted you like I did. I'm Ellanece Mosley, the owner of this house, come, let's get you settled and we'll discuss work hours and what not." Justin grabbed his two suitcases out of the bed of his truck, and followed the woman, as she made her way around the house, to the front door.

Ellanece enjoyed watching his jaw drop as he gave the place a good look over. "How old is this place?" he asked. She replied, "Oh it's *old*! Early nineteen-hundreds old, and last time this place was remodeled was probably late nineteen-fifties or early sixties." The two walked up onto the porch of the home and Justin asked another question, "How much did you pay for this place?"

Smiling as she unlocked the front door, she answered, "Not that it's any of your business, but I bought it off auction for a cool forty grand. The

place was a real *shit-hole* when I first got it." Justin
closed the door behind them and said, "Sounds like
a damn good deal!" Ellanece shook her head all the
while still smiling and answered, "Sure, I suppose
you could say that." Ellanece continued to give
Justin the grand tour of the place, explaining in
every room the things that she had fixed or
replaced, and how much of a pain in the ass it was
to do so.

As they finished up, she brought him back to
the room that would be his, stating, "Sorry for the
lack of furniture in the place, I originally was
intending on having to shack up with anybody. Got
the cot from a thrift store, along with the pillow and
sheets, sorry if they have any stains on them. The
America's Thrift Store said they came as is." She
watched as Justin lugged his large blue suitcase into
the room, and shuffle it into the corner.

"Again, apologies for lack of furnishings,
looks like the next couple of months, you're just
gonna have to live out of your suitcase. If it makes
ya feel any better, I've had to do it before too. Shit
sucks...I know. Best thing to do is make three piles:
Clean, *kinda clean*, and dirty." Justin made a three-
sixty observation of the room, and inquired, "So I
take it, up-stairs bathroom is mine?" to which she
scoffed, "Oh no sweetie, the master-bedroom ain't
got a bathroom, upstairs is mine, downstairs is
yours...if it's too terribly late in the night, when
nature calls, try to be as quiet as you can going up
and down them stairs."

Justin nodded his head, then paced over to
the cot and bent over to feel how comfy the thing

would be, once he determined that it wasn't, he commented, "It'll be roughing it, but hell, I came here to work not sleep, right?" she clicked her tongue, replying, "Right! So I don't know about you, but I'm starving, what do you say we go for a bite to eat?" Justin's face lit up, as he offered to drive, but Ellanece responded by dangling her keys in the air, indicating they were taking her car and they drove to Skidmore's Restaurant, for a fried chicken dinner.

After they ordered their food, the two sat down at a table across from one another, Ellanece dug through her purse, producing a prescription bottle, and tapped out two blue pills. "What are those?" Justin asked. To which Ellanece casually shrugged, "Adderall…it's for my ADHD." Justin stared at the pills grimacing, "Not to be intrusive or anything, but I've heard some bad shit about that stuff."

Ellanece shot Justin a rather put off look, and scoffed, "Yea, well they're fucking prescribed by a doctor…and trust me, I'm basically a dysfunctional cunt without 'em." Justin shook his head, "I've just never seen anybody take two of a prescribed dosage. What are they 5 or 10 mg's?" Snickering to herself, she popped the pills, and as she swallowed, she replied, "Hell no, they're 40's"

"Jesus Christ! There's no way any doctor prescribes 80 mg of Adderall to a patient!" Ellanece smiled, stating, "You're right, I'm only supposed to take one a day. But you see, normally I also pop an unprescribed Lexapro pill, and the guy that usually gets those to me is out, so I'm subbing the second dose of Adderall for the Lexapro."

An awkward silence fell between the two, and Ellanece felt that this would be a good time to get to know the guy a little bit. "So Justin, I just wanted you to know that it was pretty cool of you to agree to just up and leave Jackson at a moment's notice, to hop on a job for your boss."

"Yea well, that's how you get ahead in life; you gotta be ambitious and be willing to do the things that other folks won't. To be honest with you, I was just stoked that Mr. Clarke trusted me enough to come out and head this job up for him. I've only worked for him, for a little over a year." Ellanece was unintentionally playing with her hair, which Justin automatically assumed, she may be flirting with him. Trying to keep the conversation flowing, she asked, "So how old are you?" Justin blushed and answered, "Nineteen."

Shocked at what she had just heard; she was quick to bring her hands up to cover her awe-dropped jaw. "Oh my goodness! *You're a goddamn baby*! Well I guess it's a good thing I asked, I was about to ask ya if you wanted to go out for a beer before turning in." Justin shrugged and was now blushing even more, and said, "Hey if you're offering, I've never turned down a free beer before."

Ellanece playfully swatted at him and said, "Stop! First of all, I will not contribute to the delinquency of a minor. Second of all, I'm now embarrassed that I didn't already know." Curious as to just how old he thought she had mistaken him for, he inquired, "So—just how old do I look?"

"I dunno, last time I hung around a nineteen-year-old, I was also nineteen, I just thought that maybe you were just really young looking for your age; and as it would turn out, you're just really young." An employee served them their food, and before chomping into his chicken fingers Justin added, "Well, just so we're clear I'm a grown man, I can take care of myself, and I don't want you thinking that you are going to have to babysit me or anything."

She took the first bite of her food while rolling her eyes at how good it was; and as she finished chewing and swallowing her food, she reassured him, "Mr. Howard, as long as you finish the job in decent amount of time, and help me finish my home before the next few months is up, I'll treat you exactly how you want to be treated." ending her sentence with a wink. The two continued on with casual conversation, they finished up their chicken and fries, and afterwards, they turned in to 300 East Church Street to wind down for the night.

Chapter VIII

A Mid-Summer's Fling

The next morning, Ellanece was sitting at her kitchen table, enjoying a cup of coffee with her iPhone, scrolling through Facebook posts, till she heard Justin shuffling down the stairs. She got up from where she was seated, making her way to the coffee maker, and poured him and herself a cup. "Mornin' Ms. Mosley," a smile graced her face and she replied, "Good morning, indeed, come on in." Justin slowly trudged into the kitchen, and Ellanece handed him the warm cup of java. "So, where do you want me to start?" he asked.

She held a finger up to him and explained, "Well the two most tedious rooms are going to be here in the kitchen, and the living room. When it comes to the kitchen, one of the most important parts is going to be the cupboards. You see just a few weeks ago, I had a couple of Latino gentlemen, come in and remove all of the old ones and install new ones." Justin nodded, "Yes, you explained all of that yesterday, when you walked me though the house."

Pinching the bridge of her nose she shook her head, "Of course, my bad. You see! This is *exactly* what I was talking about yesterday, I haven't had any of my Adderall yet, and the two I popped at dinner wore off a few hours ago. I'm telling ya, give me a few more hours and I'll be completely useless. Anyway, getting back on track, ever since they got them installed, I've been struggling with whether or not I want them stained, or painted?" Taking a moment to look at them really good, Justin answered, "If it were me, I'd have 'em stained." Nodding her head, while tapping her finger on her chin she replied, "Hmm, interesting, and if you stained them, what shade would you go with?"

Justin took another minute to think then said, "I'd probably go with a natural oak stain, you know—keeps the mood light." Ellanece looked to Justin, clasping her hands together, resting them under her chin and said, "You're the professional!" She then walked over to where she had been sitting, and opened a binder, which contained a sheet of paper, she walked the sheet of paper over to Justin, and explained, "Okay, so I've got pretty much a basic idea of the color scheme that I would like to see in each room. If you think you have anything to add or take away, that's great, but run it by me before you commit to anything."

Ellanece pulled the collar of her shirt out with her left hand, and dug into her bra, with the other, producing a key. "Here's the key to the house, if for whatever reason you have to leave while I'm gone, just make sure you lock everything up."

For almost three weeks those were the two rooms that he worked on; while Justin painstakingly sanded and installed crown-moldings for the ceilings, and floor lines Ellanece fooled with matching curtains and drapes to all the different paint colors that she had chosen for each room. At the end of each day, the two would sit out on the front porch, and talk about all of the things they had accomplished for the day, and everything that they wanted to get done for the next.

At the end of the third week, on a Friday afternoon as they were finishing up, Justin was sitting out on the front porch resting, sipping on a Gatorade, and wiping as much sweat as he could, off of his face. Ellanece walked out onto the porch, holding two Budweiser's in her hand. She plopped down next to him and offered him one, "Here, have one of these, it'll refresh you a hell of a lot better than that juice-shit will. Trust me, you'd be surprised."

Justin sat his Gatorade down, and hesitantly accepted the beer. He then watched as she dug in her pocket, retrieving a single 40 mg Adderall pill, and washed it back into her mouth with a swig of beer, he shook his head, looked at his beer and stated, "What was all that rambling on about *not contributing to the delinquency of a minor*?"

Ellanece noticed a bead of sweat rolling down his neck, onto the shoulder strap of his wife-beater. "Dude, you've been busting your ass over here for me, and like you said, *you ain't a boy, you're a man*, and you sure as hell have been a hardworking man, and hardworking men, deserve a beer, at the end of a long day."

Justin raised his beer and took a sip and said, "So is this gonna be a new everyday thing now?" chuckling as she also took another hit, she replied. "Don't press your luck—dude. Only reason I'm letting you get by with one of my beers, is because we've completed the living room and the kitchen. The only rooms we have left, on this floor, are the sun room, and the downstairs bedrooms. Ugh, then onto the upstairs, and then the real bitch, being the entire outside."

He nodded, adding, "That really will be a bitch, because, I'm gonna have to pressure wash before I start my primer base, and it's gonna take a couple of days for the wood to dry." Ellanece winced her eyes shrugging, "After all of that, the place should be pretty much done, and ready for the market."

Justin bent his head down, and placed the bottom of his ice-cold beer onto the back of his neck, Ellanece sat in an almost trance-like-state gazing, as every last drip of water ran down, rolling over his muscular shoulders. Justin caught her looking, and when Ellanece realized she had been caught, she looked at him like he was stupid and said, "*What*? I've seen you checking me out before; don't think I don't get to take a look for myself, from time to time." Justin smiled and said, "Yea, but it's different when I do it."

She playfully swatted him on the back of the head, "Whoa! Double standard buddy, you best believe, that if you can check my ass out when I'm bent over I can take a moment to enjoy every last bit of sweat that rolls over them rippling pectorals that you got." Justin sat his beer down and with his right hand, reached over to his left shoulder and began rubbing it and said, "I don't know about rippling, *aching* is more like it."

Ellanece, who was sitting one step above Justin, spread her legs, and patted in between them and said, "Here, pop-a-squat, and I'll give ya a little shoulder massage. Loving the idea of a shoulder rub, Justin was quick to shoot up and relocate in between her cool pasty white thighs. Ellanece started by slowly rolling the bottom of her beer bottle back and forth across his shoulders. She then brought the bottle up to take another swig and set it down beside her, using both of her hands to start digging down, deep into the guy's tight sore shoulders.

Justin couldn't help but let out a slow moan of relief, as Ellanece worked her way from his shoulders, to each of his large biceps; Ellanece taking in more than just a little pleasure as she rubbed her hands over his body. "It's kinda weird though—" Justin said, not saying anything else, just waiting for Ellanece to reply, "What's weird?" she asked. He retorted, "Oh you know, the whole you checking me out deal, I mean aren't you like—old enough to be my mom or something?"

Offended at what he had just said, Ellanece broke from rubbing his shoulders and in an offended tone exclaimed, "I'm twenty-eight years old, thank you very much, I'm not even a full ten years older than you." Justin smiled and looked back and up at her and said, "I knew you couldn't be older than thirty, I just wasn't sure what part of twenty you were in.

You like how I just found out without bluntly asking your age?" Ellanece smiled and returned to rubbing his shoulders. Shaking her head at how he had just played her. "Think you're some *hot shit* don't ya." Justin turned his head to look back up at Ellanece and with a smile he said, "Awe don't be like that Ms. Mosley, you're just mad 'cause I tricked ya, into telling me your actual age."

The two stayed silently locked in a stare for a moment, and Ellanece found that her hand had moved from rubbing his shoulder, to gently stroking his face. She now found herself almost helplessly leaning over him staring into his misty gray eyes. She wasn't the only one, who wanted a kiss, he too found himself pushing himself up to try and get close, the two of them in an uncontrollable, gravitational pull towards one another, till the end result was their faces slowly colliding and their lips becoming locked with one another.

After embracing each other in a kiss for several minutes, they broke away and repositioned themselves. Justin got up, turning himself around, Ellanece tried to get up, but he was too quick for her, and he got on top of her, pinning her down to the front porch. He placed a hand, behind the back of her head, to help cushion it from the hard wood flooring, and the two began to make out once again.

It wasn't long before passing vehicles began honking at them, yelling at them, reminding them they were in a neighborhood, where children were out and about playing. Ellanece placed both of her hands on Justin's chest gently pushing to get him to break away. "Ms. Mosley?"

"Come on, let's take this inside, before the whole neighborhood, decides to boycott us. They both scrambled to their feet, and shuffled their way inside the home. With the front door slamming behind them, Justin pushed up against Ellanece, slamming her into a wall, and pinning her there, placing his hands on her hips, eventually working his hands around her hips, so that he could grab her ass and pull her in closer to him.

She broke away from kissing him a second time, and said, "You know babe—when I said indoors—I meant my bedroom." As he heard her say the words *bedroom,* a smile broke on his face, spanning from ear to ear, and he replied, "*Yes ma'am*" He picked her up, slung her over his shoulders and carried her all the way up to her room where he tossed her onto her bed, and as she landed with a bounce he said to her, "Ms. Mosley you're so fuckin' hot right now! I mean I always thought you were cute and good looking, but goddamn!"

Ellanece crossed her legs and with a mischievous smirk on her face, she said, "Well babe, if you ever plan on using that *hard on*, on me. I suggest you stop calling me *Ms. Mosley* and just call me *Ella.*" Justin cleared his throat, and he said, "You got it Ms. Ella."

To which Ellanece was very quick to throw a finger up and correct him, "Wrong! No Miss. just *Ella*—Ms. Ella is too…*cougarish*; and I'm not old enough to be a *cougar.*" All Justin could do was just stand there, awkwardly, not really knowing where to go from there. Ellanece realizing his cluelessness, she opened her legs and waved him over to the bed, "Well come on; before the moment is totally gone."

Justin made his way over to the bed, Ellanece pulling him down onto her, as they continued to make-out, she slid her hands down into his pants and said to him, "you know babe, it's generally the guy's job to make it to third base first." Justin blushed and with a nervous giggle he replied, "And ain't it usually the guy who is supposed to be older than the girl?"

Squeezing her hand around a particular organ in his pants, every other muscle except for that one, went limp in the man's body, causing him to collapse on top of her. She looked to Justin with a smile and in a surprised tone said, "Oh my word! This is your *first time*, ain't it?"

Justin blushed in embarrassment and nodded his head yes. The smile on Ellanece's face, turned slightly devious and she rolled him over onto his back, and straddled him, all the while keeping that same hand in is pants, and as she rocked back and forth she said to him, "Don't you worry *boy*, I'm gonna turn you into a *real man* tonight!"

The next morning, when Ellanece awoke, she was more than happy to see her nineteen-year-old lay, from the previous night, still in bed beside her. Normally, Ellanece only slept with men for one of two reasons, as an outlet to just blow off some steam, or to use them to her advantage, there was always an ulterior motive whenever Ellanece went out looking to knock boots with a guy.

Originally she had only come on to Justin because she was bored, and was feeling a little frisky. But when she had discovered that he was a virgin, a deviant notion had overcome her; she was thrilled and even more turned on at the thought of taking something from him that he would never be able to get back.

Just as that same, *something*, had been stolen from her, when she had been a teenager. She laid there, watching him sleep beside her, all the while holding a frolicsome smile on her face and gently stroking his hair back. The next couple of days followed like this: Ellanece and Justin would start work around their set time of nine am and would finish up between five or five thirty pm, Ellanece would offer him a beer, then afterwards, they would end the rest of the day, by passionately going at each other, in between the sheets of Ellanece's bed.

Chapter IX

An Unexpected Visit

One afternoon, shortly after Ellanece and Justin had started their little affair, Mr. Clarke, decided that he would stop by, to see how his Protégé, Mr. Howard, was fairing on his first major solo project. As he got out of his vehicle and approached the house, he could hear the deafening sound of Metallica's, *Enter Sandman*, as he approached the front door, he knocked and waited, peaking in through the glass, to see if he could see anybody, the only sign that anyone was even home, was the sound of the music blasting.

Farrington gently placed a hand to the door handle and tried to turn it, the knob tuned and he gently pushed his weight into the door and the door slowly opened. He called out, "Hello, is anybody home?" He heard some commotion coming from the room, off to his right, as he entered from the foyer into the living room; he heard a loud clatter, followed by the sound of someone cursing. He knocked on the door frame to the room, and as he peaked in, he saw Ellanece fooling with trying to hang a mirror.

After Ellanece had heard him knock and she turned to look to see who it was, she instantly dropped everything that she was doing and as she smiled and greeted Mr. Clarke, she then continued to make her way into the living room with him, where her iPhone was hooked up, to a radio docking station and killed the blaring metal music. As the music died, they both heard Justin yelling from upstairs, "Hey, why'd ya kill the music?"

Ellanece rolled her eyes and while silently holding a finger up to her lips, she winked at Mr. Clarke, and yelled out, "Your boss, Mr. Clarke, is here, and says you best get your *ass* down here 'cause you're in a heap a trouble." They heard sounds of items being dropped and kicked to the side shortly followed by the sounds of thunderous footsteps scrambling to the staircase, where Justin miraculously shuffled down them, without falling and hurting himself.

As he safely made it down, to meet with Mr. Clarke, he was slightly confused seeing both his boss and Ellanece trying their best, to hide a smile from him. "What?" he asked, "What'd I do?" Both Ellanece and Farrington, couldn't help but laugh, and Mr. Clarke, gave Justin a few hardy slaps on the back, and said, "You're not in any trouble boy, Ms. Mosley was just pulling your leg," Justin let out a sigh of relief, and Mr. Clarke continued, "Yea, I was just passing through; tending to some family related issues, and Ms. Mosley, had given me the address, in one of our e-mails. So, I figured since I was in the neighborhood, I'd type the address into my Garmin and see how my boy is doing on his first big project."

Excited that he was going to have the opportunity to give his boss a sneak peek at everything he had accomplished, Justin was quick to put an arm around Mr. Clarke, saying, "Awesome! I've completed the entire downstairs and am now working on the upstairs, after I am finished there, I will make my way to the outside. Come, and I'll give you the grand tour of the place."

Ellanece smiled at how eager Justin was to show off all of his hard work and returned to what she had been doing before, as the two men started walking around the house, discussing the colors that had been chosen, along with the crown molding that had been used. After about forty-five minutes of examining each room in the house, even the ones that hadn't yet been started on, Farrington was more than pleased with all that Justin had accomplished.

Before leaving, Farrington made it a point to get with Ellanece and discuss how impressed he was with how much Justin had gotten done, within the time frame he had done it in, and said that if he kept it up, that he should be done by the middle of the next month. Ellanece told him that she was also pleased with the work that he was doing, and was glad that they had been able to make the arrangement work, the way that they had. They shook hands and Farrington left.

As the day came to an end, Ellanece and Justin finished their day, like they normally did; out on the front porch enjoying a cold one. They sat there talking about what they normally chatted about, work related issues, along with random personal inquiries of some kind. Then they got onto the topic of Mr. Clarke, randomly stopping by. "You did well today Justin, I'm glad that you knew better than to act all sweet on me, or anything like that, in front of Farrington."

Justin shrugged, trying to play it cool, while taking a swig of his beer, and as he swallowed, he said, "Yea, I'm not really all that certain of how he would have taken it. I mean, I might tell him after we're done, ya know—especially if we continue seeing each other and what not."

After hearing what she had just heard Justin say, she was quick to throw a hand up and stop him, "Justin… sweetie. I thought I had made myself clear, that we are not dating; we are simply two people that work together, that use sex as an outlet, to blow off some stress. After we're done here, you and I go our separate ways— most likely to never see each other again."

Justin nodded, still trying to play it off cool, "Yea, yea—I know. I was just talking about how, ya know—we're now friends on Facebook, and maybe if we ever happened to be in the same town, we could hook up, or something."

"Awe baby, *look*, the only reason we are friends on Facebook is because you sent me the request, on like, the second day you began working with me; and not wanting to hurt your feelings or seem like a cold hearted bitch I accepted. Look hon, I love what we have going on right now. Let's not let feelings get in the way and ruin it for us, I promise you only feel the way you are feeling right now, because I'm your first.

"Trust me, once you bang the brains out of a couple of more girls, I'll be nothing more than the first notch on what I am sure to be a very long belt. A silence came over the two, neither one of them really knowing where to go from there. Not wanting to end the day on a silent note Ellanece started brainstorming with herself on non-awkward topics that the two of them could talk about.

After repetitively hitting back on Mr. Clarke's surprise visit. She asked, "So how many more surprise visits, do you think that we will get from ole *boss man*?" after chugging his last bit of beer, he replied, "Awe, there's no telling. 'Bout the way that man's schedule is, probably a few if any. I seriously think he just happened to be in the neighborhood."

Ellanece giggled and in flirtatious manner looked over to Justin and said, "Well, all things considered I guess it's a good thing he didn't walk in on us fuckin' like a couple jackrabbits." Justin nodded in agreement and let out a slight laugh, nervously not knowing how he should respond to the situation. Ellanece continued by saying, "You know speaking of—after having this beer, I been getting a little hot myself, think you might be down to run upstairs and play between the sheets with me?"

"You serious?" he asked.

"Baby—if I wasn't sincerely turned on, I wouldn't be asking you for sex, you wanna *play* or not?" Even though his feelings had been hurt, after she had told him that they had absolutely no future with one another; still being a nineteen-year-old, he found himself incapable of turning down a chance to get laid.

After they finished making love with one another, they laid in Ellanece's bed, cuddling together; she was gently running her fingers through his hair, putting him on the brink of a post-coital-coma. "I'm kinda curious," she said, "me knowing how much I pay your boss, for you to come out here and do this job for me; I can't help but wonder, how much your boss is paying you?"

Smacking his lips together, trying to wake up, so he could coherently answer the question at hand, Justin replied, "I dunno what you mean? I don't get paid like he does, I get paid by the hours of work I put in; that's why you're 'sposed to keep a log, of how many hours I work." Being caught a little off guard that she had forgotten to ever log his hours; she hid her mistake by saying, "Well don't you worry babe, I been logging 'em down. And since you been such a sweet heart and all, I been given you a few extra hours here and there."

"Awe thanks," he replied, "I sure appreciate you doing that for me."

"Come on now Justin. You ought to know better than that. You know Imma treat you right. Again though, out of curiosity, 'bout how much you get paid per hour?" Justin was now stretching, realizing that she wasn't about to let him doze off right away. "Mm when I first started working for him, I was getting paid shit. Only gave me 'bout nine an hour. But ever since I done showed him how hard of a worker I am, and that I can take care of jobs all on my own, he's been giving me eleven and a quarter."

"Oh my God, that man really is making a killing off you. Babe, if I had known that you were gonna be able to do as good a job, as you been doing, and in as timely a manner as you have been doing it in. I'd a just hired ya myself and let you have all the money." Shaking his head, he replied, "That's awfully sweet of you, but it never would have worked anyway, Mr. Clarke says that he has, quote-unquote, *moonlighted me*; and that I ain't allowed to work for no one else, long as I'm working for him. He also said that if I ever quit, to go work for someone different, that if that job ever fell through, not to come crawling back, 'cause he wouldn't have me anyways."

"You realize, he only told you all that shit, to scare ya into only working for him, right?"

"Yea, but after it is all said and done, it's almost a fair trade. Mr. Clarke, is one of Jackson's most in-demand personal home painters. Not to mention, that he done taught me a whole world of techniques, that I just don't think I could have learnt anywhere else."

Another stint of silence passed between them, as they continued to lay there embracing each other, both of them randomly kissing the other, usually on the forehead or cheek. Ellanece couldn't help but feel slightly guilty for the way she had just shot Justin down, earlier, telling him that there would never be a possibility for a relationship, and she realized, that in doing so she was being no better than the jerk football player who had stolen her virginity in high school. That's when her thought process began to change, "You know, I kinda been thinking Justin,"

"Thinking about what?" he asked.

"About what we were talking about earlier, ya know, there being an, *us* after you get done painting and I flip this house."

"Look Ella, you don't have to explain, I understand. I didn't mean to come off as some pussy-whipped teenager, earlier." Ellanece popped him on the top of his head, scorning him, "I ain't once, thought of you as being whipped. You're your own man, and that's what I love about you. Also, I been thinkin'—what we got right now, is a really good situation—I can't help but wonder, what it would be like, if this is how we made our living?"

"What do you mean…I don't get it?"

"I mean, you and me, flipping houses together. I lose a lot of profit sometimes, and take some big risks hiring illegals and other independent contractors, to help me with some of the really physical shit. Plus, after the day is over, I pay 'em and then they go on home; if you stuck around, I would more than just pay you well, *way* better than what Clarke pays ya, anyway.

"Also, the icing on the cake is that you and I would be working together, allowing *us* to remain being fuck-buddies." Justin scratched his head out of being just a little confused, at all Ellanece had just thrown at him, and asked, "But even if we did that, we still wouldn't be in a relationship, would we?"

"No!" she exclaimed, "That's just it, if we were pulling a long time partnership, like that, we could totally date each other. Only reason I don't want us dating right now, is because if we only do this one house, I don't want us to get emotionally attached and wind up getting both our hearts broken."

Now being a little more intrigued at the thought of a relationship, with a woman as cool and sexy as Ellanece, Justin said solemnly, "Yea, but still. I don't think that it could work. I mean we could but, it's just that Mr. Clarke has me on a—contract. See, not having any son's, I've pretty much become the only person that works for him that he trusts to leave his business to, he hasn't taken any of the other guys in under his wing like he has me.

"After he saw all my potential, he had me sign a legal document, stating that if he taught me all of his craft and how to properly run a business, that I would step up and take over his business, after he got too old." Not getting the point, Ellanece asked, "So? You'll have me, we'll have us. You won't need Mr. Clarke or Jackson. We can do like I've been doing, and travel all over the place, flipping houses wherever there's a strong market."

"Yea, but I can't help but think what if *we* don't work out. I'm screwed then. See if I stick with Clarke, after he steps down, I get all of his old clientele. If we go off doing our own little thing; and say five, six, hell ten years down the road we don't last. Then I just screwed myself outta all them customers. And I don't know for certain what that man pulls in, when it comes to personal finances, but it's gotta be close to a hundred grand a year.

"Guess all I'm saying is—as much as I would *love* to pursue something with you, I can't do that to my future self. Giving all that up, which I know will be guaranteed to me, I just can't do it." Sad that she now realized she couldn't have Justin for her own; she began to plot. "Let's stop all this nonsense anyway and go to bed." Justin agreed and the two cuddled up as Ellanece reached over to her night stand, to turn off the lights.

Chapter X

Fun-Day for a Murder Plot

The next morning when Justin awoke, he didn't open his eyes at first; he figured if he didn't open them, then he wasn't technically awake, and that he could get away, with a few more moments of pretend sleep. However, it wasn't long before he started pondering what time it actually was, and that he needed to check his iPhone, to see the time, so that he wouldn't be late for work.

That's when it dawned on him, that he couldn't be late for work, seeing as how he was technically already at work. He opened his eyes, and reached under his belly, where he felt the warmth of his charging phone ever so slightly burning against his skin.

He pulled it out from under him, and clicked the center button, to see what time it was, the time being eight thirty in the morning, which was typical for him, to sleep until half an hour before work. He could hear the clinking of pots and pans from downstairs, in the kitchen, and he thought that it was weird, he had never figured Ellanece, to be a morning breakfast person; every other morning, there had never been any post breakfast aftermath of pots pans and dirty dishes. Justin got out of bed and lackadaisically got himself dressed to go downstairs.

Justin slowly made his way into the freshly painted white and navy blue colored kitchen, where he saw Ellanece standing over the stove, flipping an omelet in a pan. She looked over her shoulder and nodded with her head, to the makeshift table made from saw horses and plywood, and two fold out lawn chairs, and said, "Pop-a-squat, breakfast is almost ready." Justin sat down in one of the fold out chairs, surprised at what he was witnessing. He thought to himself: *Hell, a guy could get used to being treated like this*.

Ellanece soon placed two plates onto the table, the plates containing an omelet, grits, bacon, and an orange slice, for garnish. After serving the plates, she sat across the table from him and they both began to eat. Neither one of them really knowing what they should start a conversation with, Justin broke the ice, by asking, "So, 'bout what time you want me to start painting today, 'round same time?"

Placing her plasticware fork and knife on the table, she brought a napkin up to her mouth, and as she finished swallowing her food, she answered, "You know, if it's alright with you, I was kinda wondering if you might want to take a *fun-day* with me, and drive over to Meridian. They have a pretty cool mall there, along with a movie theatre. Thought maybe after we scoured the mall and got some lunch, we could catch a movie or something?" confused by her suggestion, he couldn't help but ask, "What do you mean *fun-day*? I'm kinda on a timed schedule and if I don't meet that schedule, Mr. Clarke might get mad at me and not trust me with another big job like this, for a very long while."

"What could *one day* possibly do? Besides, you're already ahead of schedule as it is. So come on, come with me to Meridian, we'll have a blast, I promise." Justin had to think for a moment. "Look Ella, if this is about last night—"

"—Why're you bringing up last night?" she interrupted, "we were just talking, after sex. We conversed over what we had going on between us and we settled on the conclusion that after we are done here, with this, then we go our separate ways." Dropping his plasticware, Justin said, "Yea, and this *fun-day*, that you are talking about taking; with all of the shopping and movies; sounds more like a date to me." a morose look fell about

Ellanece's overall attitude and as she shrugged her shoulders, she said solemnly, "Maybe that's 'cause it was 'sposed to be one. But you know what—forget about it, I'd hate for you, to fall behind on schedule." Without finishing her food, she grabbed her plate and began to make her way to the sink so she could dump it in the trash. "Wait, you haven't finished eating?" Justin called out, "I'm not hungry anymore," she replied. Justin popped up from his seat and was able to stop her, before she dumped her plate.

"Ella wait, I can tell that you really had your heart set on this day, and I guess I just thought—I dunno, that you were trying to plan this day, to try and change my mind, about me not wanting to leave C.A.R.P.S." A faint smile appeared on her face as she coquettishly batted her eyelashes, elegantly replying, "Maybe I was doing a little of that as well," she winked, while shrugging the shoulder closest to him, "still think that you might be interested in going on a *date* with me." Justin grabbed the hand that was holding the plate and pulled it away from the garbage can. He then placed his other hand on the small of her back, and kissed her softly on the mouth. As they broke from the kiss, he said, "Yea, I'm still interested."

After driving forty-five minutes in Ellanece's Firebird, they arrived at the Bonita Lakes Mall, in Meridian Mississippi. They started their *day-of-fun* off, by going to the movie theatre and seeing if there were any movies that were showing that they wanted to see. "I can't decide on whether or not I want to see *World War Z, The Lone Ranger,* or *The Conjuring.*" Justin said as he and Ellanece paced back and forth from movie poster, to movie poster. She replied, "Yea I know those do seem to be the best movies that are out right now. "Oh look," Justin said pointing his finger to a poster, "I forgot about *This is the End* being out, it's a comedy where all of Hollywood's biggest comedians play themselves, in an apocalyptic parody."

Ellanece almost instantly turned her nose up to the movie, "Nah, I hate comedies. Every now and then I'll come across a smart one that will surprise me, but for the most part, they get you by using cheap gags like showing you a hot girl's tits, or making silly faces, and God forbid the cock and drug humor. I like the first three, you mentioned; now all we have to do is figure out which genre we both like, we've got *western, action-thriller, and horror.* I'm not much of a western fan, but part of

that could be my being a girl; however, I love
Johnny Depp, so I could force myself to watch it.
Then there's the Z movie, you wouldn't happen to
like that show, *Walking Dead* by any chance, would
you?" Justin paused bending both of his knees,
while shaking both his fists at chest level and
exclaimed, "I *fucking* love that show!"

     She smiled, happy that he didn't have some,
holier than thou explanation, as to why he wouldn't
allow himself to watch the show. She then
commented, "Yea, that show is pretty bad ass. Only
reason why I asked is because I heard a review in
some magazine about how *Z* is basically a hardcore
zombie movie." With that being said, Justin
positioned himself in front of Ellanece, placing his
hands, on both of her shoulders and said, "It's done!
We are going to go watch *World War Z*, end of
discussion."

     Ellanece couldn't help but laugh at her
young lover's eagerness and so without putting up a
fight, she nodded and said, "The zombie movie it is
then! However, if I am to make it through an entire
movie, then I think we should find something to eat
first, it's eleven-thirty, so if we eat within the hour,
we could make the twelve fifteen showing and be
out by two thirtyish and then we could spend the
rest of the afternoon, *shopping*! "Daw, shopping?"
Justin nagged, in a rather painful tone. Shaking her
finger at him, demandingly, she scolded, "Hey, hey,
hey... buddy! We'll see how distraught you are,
when I'm shopping in Victoria's Secret." Justin
raised his eyebrows and the entire conflict was over.

They walked out of the theater, into the mall's food court and looked around "Alright, so our dining plans are rather limited," Said Ellanece, as they stood in the food court of the mall, "We have Sbarro, Garden & Grille, Las Fuentes, and Stir." Justin shrugged his shoulders and said, "Well I think with our time limitations the obvious choice is Sbarro." They both choked down a delicious greasy calzone.

After doing so, Ellanece brought her purse up to the table, and pulled her prescription bottle out, and tapped out two 40 mg Adderall pills, tossing them to the back of her throat, with a hard swallow. Justin gave her a concerned look, much like he had done the first time he saw her tap out that high of a dosage, however, he erased the judgmental glares, once she shot him an angry scowl. The two cleared their plates and made their way across the food court so they could catch their zombie flick.

Once the movie ended the two exited the theater, and began to walk about the mall, window shopping, all the while, avidly recapping the movie. "So since we can both agree that the best scene in the movie is when the gunman in the chopper, begins to gun down all of the zombies, crawling over one another, to climb over the walls in Israel." said Ellanece, "What would you say your least favorite scene was?"

Justin replied, almost instantly, "Dude! It totally was when Pitt, chopped that Israeli chick's hand off, after she got bit by the zombie. They *so* stole that idea from *The Walking Dead,* remember when in one of the first episodes of last season: when the walker bites Herschel on the leg, in the jail cell, and Rick comes to the rescue, by chopping off his leg; and when they asked how he knew it would stop Herschel from turning; all he said *was that he didn't*. I'm just saying, that when in the movie, they figured out the girl wasn't going to *turn*, and they asked Pitt how he knew it would work, I knew *exactly* how he was gonna respond."

They stopped outside of the store front of Victoria's Secret and Ellanece bore a devious smile, and asked, "Are you ready for me to model some very skimpy lingerie for you Mr. Howard?"   Justin responded by silently nodding his head trying to hide all of his excitement, trying to play it like the cool, experienced, *ladies-man*, that he so obviously wasn't. They entered into the store where Ellanece continued to do as she had advertised before, by displaying to Justin, articles of lingerie that she had allowed him to personally pick out. After finishing up the mini burlesque show, they continued to shop around a few other stores, Like Dillard's and J.C. Penny's.

As they walked away from the mall, to get into Ellanece's Firebird, she had bought herself two bras from the *Dream Angels Collection*, (one of which she was wearing) and Justin bought himself a blue and white Nautica Polo, just in case he wound up needing a shirt for a special occasion for the remainder of his stay in Bucksdale. All he had packed before he left were Carhartts and work shirts, not expecting to be getting involved in any romantic situations while he worked.

The drive back to Bucksdale was mostly a quiet one. Ellanece had her iPhone hooked up to the radio, and Justin was DJ-ing, mostly playing nineties hits, from artists like: *Nirvana, Soul Asylum, and Smashing Pumpkins* just to name a few. "So how would you say our date went?" Ellanece inquired. With a giant smile reaching from ear to ear, Justin replied, "I loved every moment of it, I can't wait for a second one—" An awkward moment fell, and Justin asked out of curiosity, "—there will be another date; won't there?"

She contorted her lips and after a moment of thinking she said, "I don't know, babe? I know I was really adamant, about us taking this date; but that's just because—I wanted to know what a date with you, would feel like. Just as I also wanted you to know, what it was like, to go out on a date with me. I guess my point is, if we allow a second, third, or fourth date; all we are doing is harming to ourselves, in the long run. It really all depends on you, Mr. Howard" Pointing to himself, in a surprised manner, he replied, "On me?"

"Yeah babe, you really have to choose to commit to being about *us*, and leave Mr. Clarke, and his C.A.R.P.S. or you can stick with them and forget about *us*."

"Ella I had so much fun with you today and I can't think of a cooler chick than you. But like I said, it's the money."

"Okay look at it this way, you can stay with Mr. Clarke and keep your *promised money*. Or you can come work with me, and we can make a lot of money, have a lot of fun making money, and the best part is, we also get to have a lot of fun making love, while having fun making money." Justin had never really thought about it that way, but he still had his concerns about abandoning Mr. Clarke. Ellanece could see his concern, by his furrowed brow. Not being able to stand his silence any longer she chimed in one last suggestion. "You know, there is also one other way, where you and I get to be together, have all of our sex, money, and fun; and *you* getting to *keep* all of *C.A.R.P.S* loyal customers."

"How the hell do you suppose we do that—kill him?"

"*Exactly!*"

"Ella, I was *joking!*"

"Yea, well I wasn't. Listen—just hear me out. He's already up there in age; the dude has lived his life. If we kill him, the company's not just gonna disappear, you'll be there to take over and all of his loyal customers will naturally turn to the deceased's protégé. That's business for you and me. The only part of our plan that changes is that we both stay in Mississippi instead of traveling the country; and trust me babe, I am more than willing, to make that compromise." Justin thought a moment longer, then said, "Jesus Christ Ella, those pills have gone to your fucking head—the guy has a *family*—what about *them*? It just wouldn't be fair."

"Life isn't *fair* Justin!" She exclaimed as she pulled the car over to the side of the road, "look, my head is fine, what we have is something wonderful and amazing, and we could enjoy everything about it, all the while making tons of money, but only if Clarke dies."

"So wa-wa-what are you suggesting? That we just invite him over and shoot him in the face, or something?"

"No babe! That's too direct; we'd get caught for sure. If we were to go through with all of this, then we would have to be subtle about it. Ya know, make it look like an *accident*." Turning his head to look out the passenger side window of the car, he solemnly asked, "And just how do you suppose we do that?" Ellanece smiled and as she placed the car back in gear, to get back onto the road, she replied, "We'll discuss it more, once we've gotten back home."

Ellanece and Justin entered in, through the back door, of her house, both of them holding a brown paper sack filled with groceries, and their items, that they had purchased at the mall. As Justin turned to close the door, the town's church bells could be heard in the distance, informing people that they had just embarked upon a new hour of the day. Four o'clock pm to be exact.

They entered into the kitchen and set the bags they had been carrying, onto the makeshift kitchen table. Ellanece reached down into the sack, that she had been carrying and pulled out a six pack of Budweiser, a pack of Hebrew Nationals, and some Wonder Bread hot dog buns. Justin had taken a seat at the makeshift table and had become immersed in his Facebook account on his iPhone. Ellanece looked over to him and rolled her eyes and then continued pulling items out of the bag that he had been carrying.

After putting everything up, she began to prepare for dinner. She pulled out a pot, filled it with water and flung three hotdogs into the pot. One for her and two for Justin, she then crossed over to the cupboard, pulled out a large bowl and filled it full of chips and placed it onto the table right in front of where Justin sat. While she waited for the dogs to finish cooking, she walked over to Justin and began to rub his shoulders.

They had for the most part been completely silent, ever since she had told him that they would finish conferring, on how to make Mr. Clarke's death, appear to be an accident. Letting out a slight moan of ecstasy, Justin said to her, "Mm yea, that's the spot; right there."

She smiled faintly and said to her companion, "Oh don't mind me, I'm just tending to my womanly duties as your *girlfriend*. You know; things like makin' your supper, and rubbing your sore shoulders. Now why don't you just go ahead and complete the trifecta you got going on here and lean that head of yours back into my chest. Doing as he was told, he smiled as he was now completely relaxed.

The timer for the dogs went off and she was forced to quit rubbing him, so that she could fix them, their plates. "How do you like your dogs prepared?" she asked.

"Just mustard and ketchup, please," she nodded at his request and after a short while she placed both plates onto the table. She then crossed to the fridge and retrieved two beers from it. She placed one in front of her lover and the other one stayed with her. She took her seat across the table from him and as she bit into her hotdog she kept her eyes fixated on Justin. She swallowed her food and took a sip of her beer and asked, "So, have you given any more thought as to what we were talking about earlier?"

"You mean about Mr. Clarke?"

"Yea,"

"Well—I'm not gonna lie, I must admit, it does disturb me just a little, that I have even given it a second thought. But also, I can't help but think you seem to be awfully confident that we can do this and get away with it. It's almost as if you've done this sort of thing before."

She calmly took another bite of her hotdog, all the while still keeping her gaze fixated on Justin. She slowly chewed the rest of her bite and calmly went for another sip of her beer, as she contemplated the lie that she was about to prevaricate for him. "Justin," she said, as she wiped the corners of her mouth with a napkin, "I thought I had told you, about the man that I killed, after he more or less broke into my home, to try and rape me." Justin slowly shook his head, "Naw, this is different.

What you did there, was a natural self-defense reaction. What you're doing now is premeditating, and you're plotting this entire shit out; like you have done this more than a couple of times." Ellanece took in a deep equable breath, and replied, "Okay, you're right. But what I'm about to tell you, is probably the deepest darkest thing that has ever happened to me; and you have to promise me that everything I'm about to tell you, stays between you and me. If you can't do that, then I guess we really don't have a future together and you can pack your things to go back to Mr. Clarke and I'll just have to find me another painter, to help me finish the house."

Justin grabbed his napkin out of his lap and violently threw it on the table and said, "No Ella. I promise you, whatever you tell me will not leave this room, but I can also assure you, that what you tell me, determines on whether I stay or not. So by all means—go ahead and tell me what you got to say." She went for another sip of her beer, and as she set the cold sweaty bottle down on the makeshift table top, she began to tell her story.

"You see, I've been in only one other situation, where it benefitted me to have another human being gone from this earth."

"So you mean to tell me that you have only killed *two people*, throughout your entire life, once in self-defense, and the other in premeditated murder?" Ellanece slowly nodded her head, "Look babe, it's *life*, it's just the way things are in this world, you're born, you grow up, and after a certain point in time in your life, you have to make the cognizant decision that you are here to play the game of life, and sometimes, the game of life, calls for a little bit of *murder*. I was just a little older than you are now, I was twenty-two, and I had just started my career, in realty.

"I come from a family of realtors, so naturally, my first job was with my aunt and uncle; which would have been an awesome experience, if my bitch of an older sister, (whom they favored over me) hadn't worked there as well. You see—the way things worked, was like this: My aunt and uncle owned their own company called Mosley and Co. Realty. And we'll just say that their business was to them, what Clarke's business is to him.

"Anyway, my aunt and uncle, would sit with the clients individually and get to know things like, what kind of budget they had their minds on, which school districts that they want their children to attend, if they wanted to live in the same neighborhood as the church they belonged to, or even if they wanted fast and easy interstate access.

"But fuck it, whatever…to make a long story short: My sister, being the favorite, got all of the wealthy, high-end clients that were looking for rich prominent neighborhoods. While I on the other hand, got all of the low-income families, that either had to settle for post WWII homes, duplexes, or small but quaint garden homes. She easily turned two sometimes three hundred thousand a year; whereas I was usually bringing home anywhere from forty to sixty thousand a year."

A silence passed through the room as Ellanece was curious to see how Justin was going to react to the fictitious tale that she had begun to feed him. Justin took a few swigs of his beer and after swallowing, he said, "Are you implying that you whacked your older sister all because she made more money than you?" Ellanece shook her head and replied, "I know how all of this must sound, and I also realize how shallow, I must be making myself out to be; but you have to realize, they never threw me a bone. All the good clients went to her, every *fucking* time!"

Justin tossed his head back chuckling, "Ella, do you even realize how ridiculous it is, that you were twenty-two, twenty-three years of age, making forty to sixty a year? I mean I realize I'm only nineteen, working as a painter, but I'm lucky if I break over twenty thousand a year. Sixty, for a person in their early twenty's, is doing pretty damn well for themselves!"

She nodded then continued, "Yes but you have got to understand, that it is so much different, when sibling rivalry is involved. Can you even imagine, just for one second, what it would be like if you had an older brother, and you both worked for Mr. Clarke, the only difference being, that when you both showed up for work, he pulled up in a brand new Mercedes, while you pulled up in a brand new Kia. All the while keeping in mind that as y'all both worked throughout your day, he would be getting paid, three times as much as you, just so he could work in cushier more comfortable conditions, with half of the stress. Admit it; you'd be a little pissed."

The corners of Justin's mouth turned, forming an upside down U, and with a nod of acquiescence, he replied, "You know what, now that you put it that way, you're right. I would totally be pissed at the guy; as a matter of fact, I would be so upset with him, that every morning when I walked by his fancy new Mercedes, I would drag the key to my humble new Kia down the side of his Benz—but I wouldn't *fucking* kill him—he's my brother." Realizing that she was on the verge of losing him, she carried on with her story, "Yea well, you and your fictitious brother obviously have a better relationship than me and my late tangible sister."

"So how exactly did you go about killing her?"

"Ricin,"

"The hell is ricin?"

"It's a highly potent poison that comes from castor beans. A dose the size of a few grains of table salt, can kill a person, if it's: injected, inhaled, or digested… let's just say one night I had my sister over for some dinner."

Justin scratched his head, out of confusion and asked, "Okay, but if ricin is so potent and you put it in the lasagna, how come you didn't die as well?"

Ellanece smiled and with charming tilt of the head, she replied, "The poison was on the plate, not in the food; and my sister while not being a fat or large woman, as you can tell by my framing, she was an avid foodie. She also loved my lasagna and whenever I prepared it for her; she would always playfully lick the plate clean. Not that she would have had to do that, to die from it anyway, but it was a good reassurance that the bitch would drop dead."

Justin got up and slowly paced back and forth, running his hands through his hair trying to figure out, just how exactly he should be reacting, to everything Ellanece was telling him, "How long did it take for her to die?" he asked. "She was dead within the night, probably within the first few hours of her returning home, she had already begun to bare the symptoms, before she left. As she got into her car she mentioned feeling a little nauseous and about three hours after she got home, she sent me a final text, jokingly cursing me and my delicious meal that I had prepared for her, and that she was experiencing *Montezuma's Revenge*."

Justin had stopped pacing was now using his elbows to prop himself up on the table, as he clung to every word that she said, curiosity got the better of him, as Ellanece was taking another long pause from her story, he asked, "Is that how she died, diarrhea?" Coughing to clear her throat, and as she did so, her lips tightened and she slightly turned her head away from Justin, so that she wouldn't have to look him in the eye, "No," she said, "diarrhea is only one of the first symptoms, ricin usually takes a couple of days to kill a person but in my sister's unfortunate case, she died that night.

"You see, the way ricin works is like this, after the first common symptoms occur, which most people could pass off as a stomach bug or eating a bad batch of food; later the symptoms become more hardcore, like hallucinations and seizures, usually after the seizures ensue, one would be admitted to a hospital, where eventually, if the doctors weren't able to figure out the cause, of all that was taking place, the victim's liver, spleen, and kidneys would give out within the week."

"How did you know that the doctors wouldn't figure out she had been poisoned with ricin?"

"Ricin is the kind of poison that's used by terrorists, to kill off politicians that they don't like, or highly disagree with. My sister was a twenty-seven-year-old, real estate mogul, whom everybody loved, and enjoyed to be around. Ricin would have never crossed their minds. Not to mention that even if they had guessed what it was; it's not like it would have made a difference. My sister died that night. She wound up having a seizure and since she lived alone, there was no one there to stop her from swallowing her tongue."

The look on Justin's face was a mixture of great horror and amazement, "I must admit," he said, "my mind, has just been completely fucking blown. When we first started having this conversation, I had no idea how *educational* it was actually going to be. I couldn't help but think, that you were gonna tell me, you hired a hit-man, or cut her brakes, hit her in the head with a hammer, you know—the *normal* shit folks think up to kill other people.

"Which brings me to my next question, Ella, how in God's name could you, at the age of twenty-two, have had all that knowledge on ricin, and how effective it would be? I mean if I had never had this conversation with you, I would have probably never learned all of that stuff. I mean that's the kind of shit, that like you said, terrorists and doctors, should only know."

Ellanece simply smiled digging into her pocket and pulled out her iPhone, which she carelessly dangled in front of her. "Ahem, little did Steve Jobs know, of the *Pandora's Box*, that he was placing into every: wannabe serial killer, jealous ex-girlfriend, and cuckolded husband's palms, when he and his company, developed the first iPhone; it's quite simple darling, I Googled potent non traceable poisons."

"Alright, my next question," he said, "seeing as how you killed your sister to get all of her high-end clients and deals, what the hell went wrong? Why are you here, instead of there?" bowing her head, almost tucking her chin to her collar bone, she brought her head up, to look at Justin, as a single, forced, tear rolled down her smooth pale cheek, she sniffed and explained, "Let's just say I didn't take murdering my sister as well as I thought I would have. I mean after all, I'm only human. I'm not some cold blooded monster. I took it pretty harshly, I never broke down bad enough to admit what I had done, but I did get pretty heavy into drugs.

"You see, other than all of the guilt, my plan had worked flawlessly. My aunt and uncle did just as I had thought they would, and they started giving me some real fat-cat customers. I made a few big deals, bought me an Audi TT. Things were going good, until my drug habits started to take their toll. Aside from upping my Adderall dosage to almost 100 mg, I got really big into, Oxy, and Xanax. Also, whenever I was off work, I drank like a fish. It was only a matter of time; before I wound up over dosing, at a party I was at, and would up being rushed to the hospital. Well needless to say, my aunt and uncle were devastated when they found out about my addictions, I tried to tell them, that it was just the way I was dealing with the loss of my sister, but they weren't hearing it.

"They wound up sending me to a six-month rehab clinic and after I finished it and was able to prove that I had truly kicked all my bad habits, they told me they had sold my TT along with a few of my other rich impulse buys and they placed thirty thousand dollars into my bank account and told me that I was on my own; that they refused to have the rich clientele that they brought in, to be my demise. They said I couldn't handle copious amounts of money very well."

"Where did you go from there?" Justin asked as he now stood behind her gently rubbing her shoulders trying to comfort her. "Well I did all I could do," she replied, "I made my way to the first used car lot I could find, bought me that Firebird and began my house flipping career."

Ellanece stood up from where she was sitting, with her arms crossed rubbing each other, she continued to take a few steps away from Justin, and she said, "You know, now that I think about it, I don't know if I could live with Mr. Clarke's death haunting you, the way that my sister's haunts me; after all, you're not even twenty."

Justin wrapped his arms around her pulling her close to him, he put his mouth to her ear and as the warm air from his breath sailed over and into the canals of her ear, he softly spoke, "Yes, but Mr. Clarke's my employer, not a blood relative.

Question: Just exactly how much money, could we actually make, if we ventured out on our own?" with one graceful motion she spun herself around tucking her arms into her chest and rested her head on Justin's shoulders and said to him, "Hundreds of thousands of dollars', baby. We're talking we could probably gross a million dollars in a four to six-year span."

"Damn," he whispered as he continued to kiss Ellanece's head, "you realize it took my old man, the better part of thirty years to make over a million dollars." She looked up to him, with her soft blue eyes, wrapping her arms around him, and with a sensual touch to her voice, she said, "We could make a lotta love and a lotta money—if you wanted to go through with this."

He squeezed Ellanece just a little tighter, bringing her in, to where he could feel her soft breasts pressing up against him, and he said in a somewhat hopeless manner, "Ella I would love nothing more than to spend the rest of my life, waking up next to you every morning, just so I could go to work with you every day, so that we could make a fortune together. It's just that deep down; I know that I just don't have it in me, to kill another man, even if he was my worst enemy, I don't know if I could do it?" She closed her eyes, and said to him, "I know that you don't have it in you, baby. That's why I'm gonna offer, to do it— that is, if you think you could live, with him passing, before his natural time?"

Justin thought for a moment and then with a nod of the head, he replied, "If him dying meant that you and I could be together with shit tons of money, then yes, I could live with his untimely passing."

"Then it's settled, we'll call him over here sometime next week, we can use the excuse that we need his opinion about something and after he gets here, I'll kill him then." Justin had a puzzled look on his face and he asked, "No offense babe, but shouldn't we like, invite him out to dinner or something? I mean it wouldn't it be pretty hard to get him to ingest ricin." Ellanece chuckled aloud, and said, "Darling, that's cute, but I don't think that I am going to be able to use ricin this time."

"Why not, it seemed to work for you pretty well last time, didn't it?" She replied with a quick nod, "Yes but you see, ricin isn't just something that you go down to the local drug store to pick up. You damn near have to be or know a chemist, in order to get that stuff, and even then, once you have it, it could wind up being, a ticking time bomb, if you are not careful with it."

His brow furrowed, and he asked, "Well then just how do you 'spose you're going to go about doing it?" She shook her head and a concerned look grew about her face, "I don't know?" she said, "I haven't really decided yet. I'll have to give it some serious thought of how I'll go about doing it, I'm going to have to make it look like an accident. I was thinking that a large fall of some sort might do the trick."

"Yea, but how's a girl your size, going to make a man his size fall to his death?"

"I was thinking that I could maybe ask for him to go up and look at something on the roof and just as he got to the top of the latter I could kick the feet of the latter out from under him." Justin shook his head, "Nah it won't work like that, Ella you can't way more than a buck ten soaking wet, and Mr. Clarke is over two hundred and fifty pounds, I don't even know if I could pull off that feat."

Ellanece's soft silky lips once again found themselves contorted upon her face, as she was now in deep thought. "You know," she chimed, "there is always the possibility of a nasty fall down the stair case. How old would you say Farrington is?" Justin threw his eyes into the corners of his head, thinking, "I should know this," he said, "I couldn't give you an exact number but he's definitely in his sixties."

"So, a nasty fall down the stairs, very well could make him a goner, couldn't it?"

"Yea, I 'spose it could."

"Yes, he would only have to fall and land in just the right way."

"But still Ella, how's a little ole thing like you, gonna push a large-ass man like him down a flight of stairs?" Ellanece thought for a moment, but before she had time to say anything, Justin said, "What if I distracted him, while you came up behind him with a rope, and strangle him?" Justin made the motions with his first of strangling an imaginary person with a rope, all Ellanece could do was just grimace, and not call him an idiot.

She continued to shake her head, replying, "No way, dude! That would totally leave ligature marks. We'd get locked up for sure. Besides, I really like the stair case idea. The only problem is that I would have to trip him, and the only way that I could do that, would be to give him enough inertia, to crack his skull and break his neck would be to use something with a hook so that I could pull—like my crowbar!"

"Baby I'm telling you, you're just not big enough."

"Don't matter the difference in size, a person's shins are one of the most sensitive parts of their body, aside from the genitals, nose, and throat. If I were to catch him right at the edge of a step then the shock of the blow would most likely cause him to jump, and once he's airborne his weight only works in my favor."

She was now standing in the doorway of the kitchen, sticking her head into the entrance of the living room, which held the stair case. Justin once again made his way back behind her, placing his hands on her hips and he said, "If you say it will work babe, I trust you." She shook her head and turned to him. "There is only one thing that I am truly worried about if we do this." Justin gently stroked her cheeks with the backs of his hands and he asked, "Yea, and what's that?"

"When I go to strike him on his shin it's going to leave one nasty bruise."

"Yea, so?"

"Baby—dead folks don't bruise like they did when they was breathin'. Every mark I make on him, while he is alive, leaves a clue that it wasn't an accident. If a coroner, or even a Detective, saw this, they'd know that fowl play was involved." He let

loose of her hips turned away and shouted,
"Dammit! No matter what we do, there is always
something that gives us away!"

Ellanece slowly began to make her way
back towards Justin. She held her hands together
pressed tightly into her stomach. On her face she
wore a very worried demeanor, and she asked,
"Baby, I need to ask a pretty serious question,
okay? You may not be able to *kill* Farrington
Clarke, but do you think you could *take the fall* for
killing him?" Justin was struck with a befuddled
look, and he asked, "Why the fuck would you ask
me that?"

"Just hear me out, I know how this all
probably sounds, but look, if I take Mr. Clarke out
this way, which I feel is the best option, given all
that we have to work with. There is about a
fifty/fifty chance, that they will find the bruise and
at the very least, will want to take us in for
questioning. If this were to happen, don't admit to
anything right away, let 'em make their rounds, at
the end of the day if they seem intent on charging
one of us, just tell them you did it."

Justin was now slowly taking a few steps
back from Ellanece, he had the gut feeling that told
him he should run, but he stuck around, for reasons
unbeknownst to him, "And why the hell would I do
that? How do you expect us to have a life together,
if I'm locked up in jail huh—conjugal visits?"
Ellanece closed her eyes and held her hands out in
front of her trying to get him to calm down. "Justin,
listen to me. I am a fully grown woman, who has
had the notion of murder, held over her head only a

few months back, if they were to charge me with murder, I would go to jail, for the rest of my life, if they didn't send me to the chair first."

"Oh—but it's okay for me to go to jail for the rest of *my* life?"

"You don't know the legal system like I do, babe."

"By all means explain, *Little Miss Lawyer*."

"Look, you're nineteen years old; in the eyes of the law, you can still appeal for youthful offender. The way the law looks at you, is that if you are over the age of eighteen, but under the age of twenty-one, you are still eligible for YO. Now, when but when you got YO, all your arrests and court hearings get sealed, and since you have no priors, your sentencing will most likely drop dramatically and if we got you a good enough lawyer, we could plead the case that you were just a nineteen-year-old kid, who is full of piss and vinegar, Farrington said something to piss you off, you acted without thinking, it's only one blow, they charge you with involuntary manslaughter.

"After all, you allegedly, just meant to hurt him, not kill him. Once again, with the right lawyer, judge will probably only sentence you to like two maybe three years in jail, with like four or five years of probation. The kicker is, that with model behavior, you would probably only serve a year, to year and a half in jail, with two to three years of probation. After all, once you are out, you and I can begin building our life together."

Justin was pacing frantically, back and forth, ringing his hands together, he stopped momentarily to say something, but changed his mind and returned to pacing. She slowly made her way to him and tried to get him to stop, because she wanted to know what he was thinking. "Talk to me!" she commanded.

He stopped in his place, and continued to charge at her, she thought of backing away, but was brave and held her ground. "The entire fucking point of us killing this guy and making it look like an accident, is so that I get to keep all his loyal customers! Now, you tell me, who the hell is going to employ, the guy who murdered their favorite home painter?" Ellanece instinctively turned on the water works to try and appeal to his softer side. "Stop yelling at me, okay," she whined as tears streamed down her cheeks, and she began breathing erratically, "I'm just throwing around ideas, so that we can be together."

She sank down to the floor, fully blubbering pawing at his pants leg, "I just wanted us to be together, that's all—that's all I ever wanted!" Hating to see a person he cared about on the floor crying, and remembering, that they were only brainstorming. he bent down and placed his arm around her, shushing her calmly; as she buried her head into his chest and began to wail as loud as she could, knowing, that he would hardly be able to bear it. He gently pulled her head up and looked her in the eyes and said, "Shush baby. Look if it means that much to you, I think I can sacrifice the business in Jackson, especially if it means a life time of making you happy." She sniffled a couple of times,

"You'd do that—why the change of heart all of a sudden?"

"Ella, I don't know what I was thinking earlier; I guess I was just being selfish. This whole conversation has been oozing with madness! No one should have to die; just so that I can have my cake and eat it too. I *love* Mr. Clarke and I suppose, I was also speaking out of selfishness, when I said that I could deal with him passing before his time. Look. As long as you are serious about making this *thing* we have—work. Then I can deal with the loss of the inheritance of C.A.R.P.S."

Chapter XI

Sex, Lies, and Murder

Moments later the door to Ellanece's room, violently swung open, and in trampled the two lovers, who were madly making out, trying as hard as they could, to tear the other's clothes off. Justin ripped Ellanece's shirt open, exposing one of the new bras, which she had purchased earlier. She removed the rest of her shirt, to better showcase it for him, but he spent little time admiring it, for it was also, quickly removed, and tossed to the floor.

Ellanece fiddled with unclasping his belt buckle, and once she succeeded, spent no time hesitating on ripping the snap open. Justin's pants hit the floor, and as he wriggled out of them, he snatched Ellanece's skirt from her waist, to the floor; then swooped her off of her feet, and body slammed her down on the bed, as they fervidly made out, on top of the covers, their remaining articles of clothing disappeared in the tangles of the sheets, and the two sweethearts began to make love. The sex was intense and filled with passion, and after they were done, the two lovers laid under the sheets, cuddling with one another, in a certain silence— both savoring the moment, in their own personal way.

Naturally, she was the one who broke the reticence; she almost always was, whenever she and he, went through any stint of quietness. "So I've been thinking... maybe I should invite Mr. Clarke over, for a late lunch this Friday? You know, so we can tell him about our plans, of you partnering up with me, after you've finished the job." Justin slowly rubbed the back of his hand up and down her arm, and then he bent his head down and kissed her shoulder, continuing to move his lips over to her ear, and whispered, "I don't know about all that... seems kinda soon."

"Well, 'bout how much time do you think you have left on painting the house?"

"One and a half—two weeks, at the most"

"Then this Friday would be a perfect time, it'd be just like putting in a two weeks' notice."

"I was kinda hoping to tell him after I was finished."

"Justin, that's a terrible idea. Look, when it comes to situations like these, the more of a notice you give, the better things will bode for you in the future. Also, I don't want you to think that you have to do this all on your own; I think that *we* should tell Mr. Clarke, together. All we have to do, is stress that it's a mutual thing, that you are going to complete the painting of my house, and that I am going to make sure, that he gets every last penny, of the money that I owe him, and we'll just play to him the old: *It just sort of happened, one thing led to another*, excuse. Plus, you never know when it comes to old timers like Clarke, given the proper notice; he might think it's kinda cute." Shrugging his shoulders, he replied, "I don't know?"

The next day, Ellanece's Firebird pulled up outside of the C.A.R.P.S. building. Her car door swung open, and as she stepped out of the vehicle, she placed both of her hands at the top of her chest and slowly ran her hands down her blouse, to smoothen out all of the wrinkles. She then continued to check herself out in her reflection in the car window, and after giving herself the, *okay*; she proceeded to march inside of the C.A.R.P.S. building.

She made a direct path for the receptionist's desk, and asked, "Excuse me Ma'am, Mr. Clarke wouldn't happen to be available would he?" the young lady looked up to Ellanece and replied, "Do you have an appointment?" brushing her hair out of her face Ellanece replied, "No Ma'am, I'm afraid I don't. You see, I'm already doing business with Mr. Clarke and I just happened to be in town, and I remembered some rather important business that I need to discuss with him."

The secretary smiled while leaning forward and asked, "May I get your last name, Miss?" rolling her eyes she replied, "Mosley, Ellanece Mosley." Smiling politely, the receptionist replied, "I'll buzz Mr. Clarke and see if we can squeeze you in. Ms. Mosley, if you'll just have a seat right over there, I'll try to get you situated as soon as possible." Ellanece smiled, nodded, and continued to take herself a seat across the room. After a ten-minute wait, which felt like a thirty minutes; the receptionist called out to Ellanece, "He's ready to see you now."

She entered into the office and took her seat in front of the desk, just like she had done a couple of weeks back. "Ms. Mosley!" Farrington belted out. "To what do I owe the Pleasure? Don't tell me that boy of mine, done tore somethin' up?" Ellanece sat in her chair with her hands clasped together with them resting neatly folded in her lap. A smile graced her face and with a tilting of her head she replied, "No, nothing of the sort. However—"

"—Uh oh," Farrington interrupted, "it's a dead giveaway, something's gone terribly wrong, when the person you are talking to, uses the word *however,* after dismissing accusations towards a certain person." Letting the rude interruption slide, she continued, "As I was saying, *however*, there is a situation, with Justin, that I think needs to be addressed; Mr. Howard and I have had *intimate relations* with one another."

"What!" he exclaimed, "Just who came onto whom exactly?" Ellanece threw her hands out in front of her, "No, you misunderstand! It was a mutual thing. I promise you. The only issue is that I intended for our little, *affair,* to be a one-time thing—twice at the most; and I know he's young, and the age difference, must be appalling to you. But you have to realize, he's a cute young stud, hanging around my house all day, painting my house, most the time shirtless. I embarrassingly enough had a few beers one day, and while being a little inebriated, I offered if he would also like few drinks. Well, one thing led to another, and before I knew it…you know the saying, *the rest is history.*"

Farrington now had a rather confused look on his face. "Ms. Mosley why exactly have you come here, to tell me that you and an employee of mine, have been having sexual relations, while he is on the job? Are you too scared to step inside a confessional?" Now sitting with her jaw dropped, she continued to roll her eyes while holding a finger to Farrington and replied, "Excuse me sir, but I am not a whore, nor am I a cougar, or some skanky hose beast.

"I am a professional realtor, who has made a sever error in judgment and I'm trying to keep Justin, from doing the same. Justin has gotten the ludicrous idea, that he would be better off quitting his job, working for you; so that he can join me in flipping houses; all in the name of having a constant piece of ass in his life."

What had once been a confused look, had now changed to a rather disturbed one. She continued, "Mr. Clarke, my intention was never to steal Justin away from you. As a matter of fact, that is the very reason why I have traveled over here; to see you. Though I am flattered by Mr. Howard's wishes, to travel with me, do business with me, all while being able to well—*do me*. I have no wishes on settling down; and even if I was, the kid's just far too young, for me. That being said, as the first woman that Justin has ever been with, physically, I don't want to just blatantly shoot him down. That's why I was hoping you could come down on Friday—to, ya know, have us a little business meeting.

"Justin will of course be completely ignorant of our meeting here today. My plan is to tell Justin, that a meeting was made between you and I over the phone, that the meeting is for him, to come out to you, about our little affair, and that he has plans to quit. You will of course disagree to this notion, and strongly advise him to reconsider. If a lengthy debate takes place, you and I can break away from the table, where you and I will walk upstairs to hash out business while Justin stays in the kitchen. You and I will supposedly 'argue' with one another, where you will enlighten me that I am wrong. You and I will proceed to come back down stairs where I will tell Justin that I am breaking off our plans and that no matter what he says I won't have him back, and that his best option for his future, is to head back to Jackson, with you."

Clarke sat with his mouth slightly open staring blankly at Ellanece. He cleared his throat and said, "Well that's one hell of an elaborate plan… you and me arguing over him, like he is some kinda property…then the two of us going upstairs and coming to a private agreement, that he is to just come back home with me. Ms. Mosley, Justin, is not a real estate deal, he's a human being with feelings.

"Feelings for you, and I'm afraid that you are just going to have to deal with that fact and break up with him on your own. My God woman! You speak as if you are a child with an overactive imagination, trying to come up with a scheme, to avoid having to pay the price." Ellanece shook her head, as if to tell him he was wrong about her intentions. "Mr. Clarke, you don't understand—"

"—No Ms. Mosley, it is you who is gravely misunderstanding her situation. Do you even know how absurd it is, that you would show up at my office, out of the blue like this, to try and hatch a scheme, to lie to your summer fling, so that you don't have to appear to him as a cold hearted bitch?

"Also, you think I was born yesterday. In order for Justin to just want to drop everything he has here, to go be with you, I don't know how long you two have been screwing around with each other, and I don't know what lies you have told that young man, but sweetie, you need to remember that at the end of the day, all you are is a piece of ass, for that boy to chase, there will be younger, hotter, sexier women than you, to enter his life, and trust me darling he will go after them, forgetting all about, little ole you."

Ellanece now sat with her head bowed as she pretended to accept the scolding that she was currently being given. She was however, upset that her plan had not worked as well as she had hoped. After a couple of more moment's gathering herself together, she arose out of her chair, looked Farrington straight in the eye, and said, "Mr. Clarke, you're absolutely right. You've successfully called me out, on my shit. Which is something not too many men, have been able to do.

"But then again, I am used to dealing with younger, hornier men, whom often fail to ever look past my tits and ass, and they usually do whatever I ask of them. I was wrong to try and play you like that, just as I am wrong for trying to play your employee, Mr. Howard. You have my word, that I will break things off in the appropriate manner."

They were now both standing and Clarke nodded to Ellanece and replied, "I'm glad to hear you say that Ms. Mosley and I promise you are making the right decision." She started to say something but then stopped, biting her lip, she then continued to say, "Mr. Clarke, I can't help but feel tremendously embarrassed, over all that has transpired today, and was wondering if you would still accept my invite, to come over to my home Friday, for lunch or dinner, which ever would work best for you? It would give you a chance to see the work your protégé has done, in person."

Presenting a slight frown all the while giving an ever slighter nod of acceptance Mr. Clarke replied, "I'll accept your invitation, but only so I can check on my employee, in person, and also, to see how many men he would need, to have the rest of your house completed by no later than Thursday, of next week."

Ellanece stuck her hand out, so that she could shake his hand, she replied, "That sounds like an excellent idea, the faster all this is over and done with, the quicker I can sell the damn place, and move on with my life." Clarke shook her hand and Ellanece exited his office, and was on her way back to Bucksdale.

Chapter XII

The Fall of Farrington Clarke Pt. II

When she arrived back home, Justin was finishing up the last room upstairs, before he moved his work, to the outside of the house. Ellanece popped in to see how he was coming along, "Sup babe? Looks like you're almost finished," she said. "Yea, I 'bout got it, just wrapping some things up. Where've you been all day?" Leaning against the door frame curling her hair around her finger she replied, "Around. Oh and while I was out, I texted Clarke to see if he was free for lunch on Friday, and he said that he could come down, but that it would be a little late, so Friday, plan for a late lunch."

"How late is late?"

"Mm one-thirty—two o'clockish, so we should probably eat a big breakfast that day."

"You asked him over so we could tell him about our plans, right?"

"Yea—but let me break the ice to him. I think if after we're done eating, I was to show him all of the work that you have done, that might distract him a little, and then I'll tell him about us, I think things will go a little bit—smoother." Justin shrugged, saying, "I don't know? I think he is going to blow up, no matter who or how it's explained."

On the Friday of Mr. Clarke's arrival, Ellanece and Justin spent the majority of the morning in preparation. The day before, she had gone out to a flea market and bought a fold out table, along with half way descent fold out chairs. Neither one of them had any real culinary experience, to prep for the luncheon; but Ellanece had plenty of experience on throwing dinner parties, on a budget.

So early Friday morning, after stopping at a Hardy's to get some sausage biscuits and OJ, they made their way over the *Piggly Wiggly* to gather some a garlic roasted chicken, store brand potato salad, a can of turnip greens, Keebler Crackers, Milo's sweet tea, and some French Onion Dip. While they were there, they also grabbed a cheap plastic table cloth, along with a sleeve of red Solo cups.

After they returned home, around eleven o'clock, Justin began setting up the table, and breaking out the plates, cups, and plasticware utensils. While Ellanece warmed the greens on the stove and had the chicken in the oven, sitting at a holding temp, so that it wouldn't fall to or below serving temperature. After everything was ready to be served the two ran upstairs to change into their business clothes.

Ellanece wore her white dress with black buttons going down the middle; the buttons ran all the way down to the middle till they were met with a black belt, which wrapped all the way around her waist. Below the belt, the dress part had been accented with black lace flowers. Justin wore the blue and white polo that he had purchased, back in Meridian, with a clean pair of Carhartts, not owning a pair of nice shoes for himself; Ellanece had gone out and bought him a cheap pair of loafers from T.J. Max, the day before.

By one thirty the two sat in the kitchen with everything ready, playing *words with friends* with one another, as they patiently awaited Mr. Clarke's arrival. Around one forty-five Justin looked out of the window and saw his boss's work truck pass by and pull into the drive way. "I'll get everything plated," instructed Ellanece, "why don't you go out there and greet your employer, and take a moment to catch up with one another." Justin Nodded and he exited out of the back door. Farrington had just gotten out of his vehicle, pulling out a nice big bottle of Pinot Grigio wine.

Ellanece peered out from the back window, as the two men met each other with a firm hand shake. Taking advantage of the time alone, she quickly crossed over to the medicine cabinet in her kitchen, opened it up and retrieved her Adderall bottle, tapping out two 40mg pills, quickly tossing them in her mouth, she once again dry swallowed them, then tapped out one last pill, and broke it in half, leaving one half in the bottle, and the other half, she swallowed, just as she had the other two.

The two men entered in, through the back entrance. As the two entered the kitchen, Ellanece stopped everything she was doing, and wiped her hands on a cloth towel, continuing to stick her hand out, for Farrington to shake. Farrington shook it reluctantly, keeping his attitude subtle, as to not aggravate the situation.

The three of them sat down to enjoy the lovely lunch. Their conversation stayed light, for the most part, mainly talking football projections for the upcoming season, how well the food was, and how every politician in the country might as well have his head stuck up his own ass. After they finished the main course Ellanece offered dessert and was relieved when everyone said that they were stuffed, mainly because, the only thing that she had, that would even come close to dessert, was tub of mixed fruit, in the fridge.

She nodded to Justin that she was about to put her plan into motion. "If ya'll want to carry the conversation into the next room," said Justin, "I don't mind cleaning up here in the kitchen, doing the dishes, it shouldn't take me long to finish up." Ellanece smiled and said, "That sounds like a wonderful idea. Mr. Clarke, why don't you follow me upstairs and I can show you the exquisite work, Mr. Howard, has done on all of the bedrooms."

Justin paused for a moment, thinking it odd that she automatically wanted to take the man upstairs, but figured he might have just been being paranoid. Farrington wiped the corners of his mouth with his napkin and scooted back from the table to stand up. "Sure—I'll bite," and as he kept an eye towards Justin he continued, "might even give us a chance to talk about some other things as well." Neither Ellanece nor Justin liked the look that Clarke had given both of them, yet they both stayed silent and acted as if they hadn't noticed it.

Ellanece and Farrington made their way up the stairs, all the while Farrington legitimately taking time to admire the architecture of the place; like the built in window cabinets built into the wall as you ascended up the stair case, which as you walked up it, took the shape of a crescent moon. They both made it to the top and Farrington pointed to a bedroom and asked, "That's the Master, right?" Ellanece nervously nodded and replied, "Yezzir 'at's my room."

As Farrington nudged the door to the bedroom open he noticed a pair of Justin's work pants and boots, resting on the floor. He turned back to look at Ellanece and said with a scowl upon his brow, "I see that you haven't broken things off with my employee, like you said that you would, Ms. Mosley." Holding both hands out in front of her, defensively, she implored, "Listen it's not that I don't intend too, it's just that I wanted to wait until he had the house finished."

"I also, see that you had every intention of sharing your filthy bed with him till that day arrived as well."

"It's not like that, I promise."

"You mean to tell me, if I go rummaging through there right now, I won't find a box of condoms?" Ellanece shook her head no, confirming that he wouldn't find anything of the sort. "No of course I wouldn't. I'm sure you're trying to get the sum-bitch, to knock you up, so he has no choice but to stay with you." Unable to control herself, Ellanece reared back and slapped him, leaving a small red patch of skin, where her hand had made contact. "What'd I tell you about callin' me a slut?" Farrington grew angry, trying to keep himself from knocking Ellanece into the wall, for striking him. "Ms. Mosley, you are what you are. We had a deal, now just because you can't hold up your end, doesn't mean I won't hold up mine. The boy and I are leaving—today! Come Monday, I'll send some men up here to finish the rest of the outside of the house. But I refuse to let you corrupt that young man, any more than you already have.

Clarke pushed passed her, walking back towards the stair case, just as Ellanece wanted him to. Ellanece hurriedly walked to catch up with him and as she passed by the bathroom, she gracefully reached inside, pulling out her crowbar, choking up on it, so the hooked part would catch his shin just right; she trotted right up behind Farrington Clarke, and as he lifted his left leg, to begin his descent; she struck the base of his right shin, with a powerful, downward golf swing.

As Clarke hopped from the shock of the impact, a yelp of pain escaped his lips. Ellanece followed through with the swing, bringing the handle of the crowbar up, causing Farrington Clarke to land on left side of his forehead, on the second step down. The weight of his body compressing on his neck, caused it to snap. On the third roll down on the seventh step, he broke a rib, causing the broken tip to puncture a lung. By the time he rolled to the landing, he had sustained three other cracked ribs, and a broken humerus, on his right arm. Ellanece heard Justin screaming from inside of the kitchen and she dropped the crowbar and scampered down the stairs.

As Justin entered in to the living room, Ellanece hopped over the corpse, trying to stop and explain to Justin. She grabbed his shirt with both hands, out of desperation. Justin, blinded by rage grabbed her with two hands and shouted, "You fucking cunt!" and shoved her down, as violently as he could. Justin came to the aid of his employer, but as he put his head to his chest to see if he was still breathing, he realized that he was too late. Justin's chest began to heave with heavy sobs of sorrow and regret. Ellanece slowly came to her feet and with great caution, began to approach Justin. "Baby— there just wasn't any other way."

Justin's sobs paused for a minute and his entire body began to shake with rage, "*There wasn't any other way?*" Ellanece knew the chance that she was taking, but she took it any way, and knelt down beside Justin, placing an arm of comfort around him. "Baby, you have to understand, I told him that you and I had been sleeping together, and that we were dating, as lovers, and Clarke didn't want to hear any of it. He called me a slut and a skank, and pushed passed me telling me that he was leaving with you today, and that he would send a crew of men to finish your job on the house on Monday."

He couldn't stop shaking his head, no. Ellanece continued with her deceitful explanation, "Baby, I chased after him and I panicked! I saw the crowbar in the bathroom and I grabbed it and swooped his feet out from under him."

A few moments of silence passed between them, "You planted it there." Justin said, quietly trying to hold back his tears. Shocked at what he had just accused her of doing, she asked "Do what baby?"

"You planted that fucking crowbar up there. I remember when we first started planning this stupid shit; about how you were gonna come up with some way of making him fall down the stairs." Ellanece closed her eyes and leaned back cursing quietly to herself. "Your right," she said in a hushed voice, "I did plant it there it was stupid of me—"

"—Stupid?" Justin interrupted, "We should have told Mr. Clarke together; and we should have done it right there, in that goddamn kitchen, while we ate lunch!" Ellanece leaned back over to Justin to try and make him feel better, by rubbing his shoulders. "You're right Justin, we should've, and that was my fault, okay! Not yours." shaking his head he replied, "Stop acting like you care that he's dead; or that I think it's my fault he's dead."

Ellanece wrapped her arms around Justin once again, despite his efforts to try and push her off of him, she put her face to his and softly kissed him on the cheek and whispered into his ear, "Stay with Mr. Clarke, I'm gonna call 911, and when they get over here I'll confess to everything." Justin looked up to her with a surprised look; he couldn't believe what he'd just heard, "I'll be right back," she said, "my phone is still in the kitchen." And she got up and walked away.

Justin turned his attention back towards Mr. Clarke, as he gazed upon the corpse; both his head and his heart were moving a mile a minute. He thought about the life that he might have had, if he had never met Ellanece, and gotten to take over C.A.R.P.S. after Clarke retired. He also thought back to the life, that he and Ellanece had planned for each other. Lastly, he thought of everything that was happening right there, in the present moment, about how Clarke was dead before him, and Ellanece was about to call the authorities, to turn herself in. He would be left with nothing and no one to turn to. He quickly rose to his feet, and decided to get Ellanece before any other mistakes were made.

As he entered into the kitchen, Ellanece had been digging through her purse chaotically, and had just gotten her hands on her iPhone. She had been moving in such a frantic manner, that she appeared to have failed to notice his presence. She swiped the lock bar on her phone and began to dial 911. She had all but the last one to press, before Justin interrupted. "Ella stop!" she froze, nervously looking up, from the screen of her phone, she asked, "Why should I? I deserve to go to jail."

"Ella baby… please, just put the phone down and let's go over our options."

"Like what? We can't just say he innocently tripped and fell down the stairs. The coroner's bound to find the bruise on his ankle; not to mention, I fucked up anyways by slapping him before I kilt him; and you—you shouldn't have to do time, for the crime, that I've done." Justin nodded in an accepting kind of manner, "That was the plan originally though, right?" Ellanece's head shook, "Justin, we wasn't thinkin' straight, babe."

"No, we were thinkin' like murderers. Like two people determined to get their way in life, now Ella, I hate that I even have to ask, but do you really love me?" She instantly dropped her phone on the table and crossed over to Justin, cupping his face, in her hands, "Baby, what kind of question is that? Of course I love you! I done kilt a man, over wanting to live a life with you. If that ain't love, then I don't know what love is?" Placing his hands on her hips he asked, "You promise that they won't send me to the chair, or sentence me to life for this."

"Baby, like I said, I don't want you having to do time for what I done."

"Yea, but if you turn yourself in, and they throw the book at you, I'm left with nothin' and nobody. At least if I take the fall, didn't you say I could get special sentencing or something, 'cause I'm under the age of twenty-one?" Ellanece wrapped her arms around Justin and gently squeezed him laying her head on his shoulders, as her body pressed up against his. "Yea," she replied in an almost whisper of a voice, "If we got you a really good lawyer, and I know a few, there's a really good chance you could serve under ten years. Depending on how we presented your case, to the detectives and to the courts, we could probably get them to charge you with manslaughter.

"Some people don't even go to jail for that. But you most likely would get sentenced to eight years; if you behaved and did time as a model citizen, you would probably only serve four of those years behind bars, the other four would either be at a halfway house, or on probation." She paused waiting to hear what sort of response she would get out of Justin, but all she got was silence, as they stood embracing each other.

Finally, Justin broke the silence, "Okay, I'll do it. I'll take the fall." She looked up at him and said, "Just know, that I would never advise you, in any way, that wouldn't be in your best interest." Justin tilted his head, and the two lovers kissed. Ellanece pushed away from him, with a let's get started, pat on the chest.

"First things first, babe; change out of those clothes, mostly though, just lose the shirt. Get your painting supplies out, and splatter some paint on your undershirt, to make it look like you've been working. We're gonna play it like this: I'm gonna call the cops, and report that I believe Mr. Clarke has passed, after a tragic fall down the stairs. Now this is crucial, don't admit to anything... at first. Let them go about making their own assumptions, as I stated earlier. Hell, ya never know, they may actually buy the theory, that the guy innocently fell to his death. Either way, don't confess till they actually have you in an interrogation room, down at the station."

"What do you want me to tell them in my confession? That you and me—"

"—Stop right there! As far as they are concerned, you and I weren't planning to do shit with one another. You mention anything about wanting to leave Clarke to come work with me; they will automatically charge us both with conspiracy, and murder." She let out a stressful sigh, and then continued, to inform him of everything that he should say, once the police got there.

"You really think that they will believe all of that?" Justin asked. Placing her hands on his shoulders for reassurance, she said, "Yes. If they don't charge you with manslaughter, they will consider it as a crime of passion; you acting out in the heat of the moment. You're young, most guys your age don't think before they act. They'll sympathize and might even put a good word in for you.

"Now, hurry up and get ready, I'm gonna wipe the crowbar down of my prints and when I call for you, you're going to need to hold it exactly as I had. After we stage everything correctly, I'm gonna call the police, we can't let that corpse sit for too long, they'll know that we've been putting a story together, and remember—only guilty people put stories together."

She quickly pecked Justin on the cheek and broke away to dart back up the stairs, while Justin followed so that he could change his shirt. After changing his shirt, he was on his way back down the stairs before Ellanece stopped him and pointed to the crowbar on the floor. "There, pick it up at the very end of the straight part, so that if you were to swing it, the hook part would catch his shin." Justin did as he was told, "Now, drop it as if you were about to run down the stairs to stop me from seeing his body." Justin looked at the crowbar for a second then tossed it down to the floor. "Great, now go set up your paint and make it look as if you've been working, I'm gonna call the authorities.

Ellanece entered back into the kitchen, and picked her phone up off of the table, where she had left it. Swiping the lock bar on the screen of her iPhone, she punched in the last one to dial 911, as the phone began to ring, an operator picked up saying, "911 what's your emergency?"

"Hi, my name is Ellanece Mosley, I live at 300 East Church Street, and there has been a tragic accident, a man has just suffered a severe fall down a flight of stairs, and is nonresponsive to anything we say to him, I would check for a pulse, but I'm scared to touch the body. Please send help—fast!"

"Yes ma'am, a unit is on its way as we speak; if you would, please, stay on the line with me, until they arrive. While you are waiting tell me exactly how he fell?" Knowing that the entire conversation was being recorded and would later be reviewed my police, she answered, "I—I don't know, I wasn't in the room when it happened. All I heard was a yelp right before I heard him crashing down the stairs." Ellanece looked out of her window and saw the flashing lights of an ambulance, "Hello operator, the paramedics have just shown up, I have to go, bye."

Chapter XIII

The Aftermath

The following days after Justin's confession, Ellanece stayed true to her word and after getting herself a lawyer, she also found a separate one for Justin. Though the Bucksdale Detectives never formally charged Ellanece with conspiracy to murder; they did make their suspicions clear, to the judge handling the case.

On Justin Howard's first court date, after he had been sworn in, the Judge asked the question if he had acted alone in the murder of Farrington Clarke, or if he had assistance from a second party? Justin firmly stated that he had acted alone, and out of anger, and that he was deeply sorry for the tragedy he committed.

A piece of him died that day, as he watched the heart broken Mrs. Clarke curse his name for his betrayal; still not wanting to believe that he had killed the man, who had once considered him to be like a son. The trial was short and speedy seeing as how he confessed to being guilty and his story lined up with all of the accounts.

Just as Ellanece had predicted, the Judge ruled the murder, to be Negligent Manslaughter, Ellanece was also correct in the assessment that Justin would be awarded Youthful-Offender status. Unfortunately, though, Ellanece had been a little light on the number of years that she predicted Justin would have to serve. The Judge not wanting Justin to feel like he had gotten away with murder, while simultaneously not wanting the Clarke family, to feel as though justice had failed. The Judge sentenced Justin Howard to fifteen to twenty years in the Mississippi State Penitentiary.

Ellanece found herself surprised, to hear the final sentencing. She had honestly thought; the Judge would have sentenced him to twenty-five to life. Deep down, she had hoped that he would get life, that way it would make it just a little easier, for her to leave him high and dry. After all, her intentions had never been to make a life with him.

Her amphetamine-warped brain had merely found itself a mid-summer fling that had gotten too emotionally complicated for her to handle. Did she love him? Sure. However, she also didn't want the burden of a long term relationship. As the Bailiff's escorted Justin from the room, he looked to his love, Ellanece, with sorrowful eyes, which wondered if he had made a mistake? Ellanece was only able to maintain eye contact for a moment,

before turning her head down to avoid the
questioning look in his eye.

Not quite sure how she was going to handle
the break up with Justin, she waited a couple of
weeks, before making the trip over to the
Mississippi State Penitentiary. Enough days for her
to hire some illegals, to finish up on the outside of
her house. Another thing that she made sure to do,
before going over to visit him, was to gather all of
his belongings into one large duffle bag, and stuff
them into the trunk of her car. As she slammed the
trunk down, she noticed a blacked out Crown
Victoria. A vehicle that she knew all too well; and it
didn't take long for Detective Jasper Lewis to come
stepping out of it.

She made her way back around to the front
of her house and back up to her porch and leaned
back against her door frame and waited for the
Detective to greet her. Lewis made his way up the
steps of her porch which was freshly painted white.
"You know something Detective? Outta all the
times I done seen you confront me, this is the first
time I noticed you ain't got that shiny ole badge on
your hip, or around your neck. If I didn't know any
better, I'd say you was here unofficially." Lewis
nodded and said, "Yes ma'am, you would be correct
in that assumption. I am merely here as concerned
citizen, Jasper Lewis."

"Don't tell me you done come over here to
try and fill the role of *Man of the House,* in Mr.
Howard's absence." Jasper angrily stuck his finger
out at Ellanece and said in a slightly angered tone,
"What the fuck have I told you about dropping the

good ole girl act with me? I know who you really are and what you are capable of."

Batting her eyelashes at him, she replied, "And just what is it that I'm so capable of, Detective?" Jasper got right up in her face and exclaimed, "I know you killed Farrington Clarke, and if I didn't know any better, I'd say you elaborately lured Dennis Henderson over here, all with the same intentions of killing him as well. There've also been reports of two Hispanic men going missing, you wouldn't have anything to do with that too would you? They were carpenters and ever since you got here you been in the business of needing someone to help you remodel this old thing...Nope, wouldn't surprise me one bit if you were the culprit!"

Rising up on her tippy toes, to get at an eye level with the Detective, and getting her lips as close to his as she could, without them actually touching, she tersely replied, "Prove. It!" Jasper took a step back and with a slight air of defeat, said, "I can't. But, don't you think, for one second, that that doesn't mean I don't see you for what you really are."

"Oh yea, and what am I, exactly?"

"You're a cold hearted, psychopathic, bitch!" Ellanece rolled her tongue around in her mouth, then exclaimed, "*Language*! I didn't know southern gentlemen knew such words."

"Don't you tell me, how to talk, in my own damn town!" Jasper peered behind him, glancing at the for sale sign in the yard. "I noticed you're finally done with all the renovations and finally got the place on the market." Ellanece confirmed with two nods of her head then curiously asked, "Yea, you interested?"

"Ya know, even though I don't have the money; if I knew it would get you outta my town any faster, I might actually buy it from ya." A faint smile appeared on her face, "And who says I'm leaving?" Sticking a finger into his chest he barked, "Me—that's who."

"And if I don't, Dictator Lewis?" a moment of silence passed between them, and in that moment Jaspers eyes shifted from left to right, before settling back onto her, "If you're not out of this town within a week of you selling this place; don't you think for one minute that I won't drive up the road to Hicksville, pick me up some meth head junkie, who the world won't even bat a second eye at if they went missing, continue to kill that junkie, and drop him off at your front door step. All the while, conveniently, being the first cop to arrive onto the scene."

She subtly shook her head, "No you won't. I don't believe you. You're not that kind of cop; and even if you were, I don't think you're smooth or clever enough to pull it off." Lewis sniffed and said, "You're right. On all fronts you are probably right. So I guess I'd just have to hire some low life bastard to do it for me." Falling short of breath, she raised her eyebrows in a surprised way and replied, "Now that—I do believe."

"Good, smart girl." He said, pointing at her, while shooting her a wink. "I can blatantly see that you and me are never gonna be *pals*, Detective, and if you want me gone, I'm gone." Without saying anything Detective Lewis slowly turned around and started to head back to his vehicle, he then stopped, as he got to the stairs, "Oh yea, and one more thing. As long as you're out of Clarke County—I don't care where you move to. That being said; I hear of any suspicious bodies—dropping *anywhere*, in the state of Mississippi, I'll come sniffing around. Now, if bodies were to begin dropping in any of the other states— well, that's none of my business. We clear?" Ellanece replied, "Crystal."

Ellanece tried to go and visit Justin the next day, to break the news to him that she wasn't going to be waiting around for him to get out of jail; unbeknownst to her, however, inmates serving time for murder were only allowed to see visitors between 9am-4pm on the second Tuesday and fourth Wednesday of every month. So she had to wait another week, for the fourth Wednesday to arrive, before she would be able to see him. When the day finally came, she was a little shocked at the change two months in the Pin had done to him.

She was sitting down at a table when he entered the room. Shaved head, beard, Orange jumpsuit, the look he held in his eyes was probably the most disturbing thing she found about him. He slowly sat down across from her and as he rested his hands on the table, she placed hers on top of his, to try and comfort him. The first minute or two they sat in silence, neither one of them knowing exactly what should be said. Justin decided he would man up, and said, "Wasn't sure I was ever gonna see you again; judging by your reaction, back in the courtroom."

"I was shocked. I honestly didn't think they would sentence you so harshly."

"They think I killed a man! Taking a man's life is a pretty fucking serious offense. And just so ya know, I don't expect this to affect you in any way, but prison—" he paused for a moment, and swallowed nervously, "— it's ten times scarier than any show I've ever watched. Pissin' and Shittin' in front of everybody. Taking showers with everybody. Constantly having to be aware of your surroundings, so you don't get got." Another silent moment passed, still not quite knowing how she should handle this situation. She knew she couldn't stay silent forever so she said, "I think I might have the place sold."

"Good, if you don't mind me asking, for how much?"

"$120,000 dollars,"

"Wow! Who finished up the outside of the house, was it you?"

"Heavens no, I hired a few illegals who did a much cheaper—much sloppier job, than you would have ever done, on the other hand though, it only took 'em two and half days. Speaking of job completions, I don't want you to think that I'm screwing you out of your share, of the profit, for all of the hard work you did. So I opened up a savings account at Wells Fargo, in your name, and placed twenty-five thousand in it. If I'm doing the math correctly, with a one percent interest rate sitting for fifteen years, plus any money, that you may leave with, when you leave here; you should have anywhere from thirty to thirty-two thousand waiting on ya."

"I still think I should've gotten more… after all, I am doing hard time for you."

"You're getting what I've already given you. Also I um, um—I most likely won't be living in the state of Mississippi much longer. So, that's gonna cut into a lot of visiting time for me."

"Are you seriously breaking up with me?"

"Look it's not so much breaking up, as it is explaining the lack of visits that you'll be receiving. You'll still see me—just not as much as you would probably like."

"Any of them visits gonna be conjugal visits?"

"Let's just play those out by ear, why don't we. I'm not quite sure where I'll be moving to, but I'm thinking Florida, or maybe even the Georgia coast, so you know a lot of planning will have to go into all that, I don't know if you can even call the prison, when you are out of state. I promise though, we can stay pen pals." Justin sat in front of her, barely even being able to stand what he was hearing. "Why ya gotta move outta Miss-sippy. Can't you make good money flipping houses here? I mean shit. Making $120,000 on a cool 40,000-dollar investment sounds good to me."

"It was more like making $75,000 dollars; you have to factor in all my *expenses*."

"Right, don't you forget now, you also got away with killing two men in that house. I didn't get to kill nobody; and I'm doing the best fifteen years of my life for it."

"Justin, look, I didn't exactly get away with it. That damn Detective Lewis somehow knows, or thinks he knows, that I killed Farrington Clarke. He told me that if I didn't move out of Mississippi he was gonna hire a hit man to have me killed." Justin had his head bowed shaking it with a sorrowful smile on his face as he slammed his fist down onto the table, he asked, "Is every word out of your mouth a fuckin' lie?" Shocked at what she was hearing she tried to defend herself by claiming, "Justin, I know it sounds farfetched, but it's the truth!"

"No it isn't! You wanna know how I know? That damn Detective Lewis paid me a visit, the first month I was in here—" Ellanece's lips began to tremble out of rage, and though they were trembling, they somehow managed to form a half crooked smile, and she said, "You. You ratted me out to him didn't you, ya little bastard. That's why he's so certain I did it."

"Not saying I did, because I didn't, but even if I had; what difference does it make? You're still the one who gets to walk out of here today. You're not the one doing fifteen-twenty years hard time for something you didn't even do." Ellanece calmly stood up, and in a soft voice, she said, "We're over. When you get out of here, don't try looking me up, it won't end well for you. Lastly, while you're serving out your time here; I hope you rot! I pray that pretty little ass of yours gets raped, beaten, every day; and if in the midst of all of that you were to contract an STD like AIDS or Syphilis... I'd laugh,"

She had wanted to add at least one more insult, but was interrupted by Justin lunging up at her, punching her in the face with a hard cold fist, breaking her nose. He tried to get a kick in, but a guard tackled him before he was able to. Another guard assisted in bringing Ellanece to her feet, and as two other guards' dragged Justin away, he yelled at the top of his lungs, "You ruined my fucking life, bitch!"

Before leaving the prison she stated that she wanted to press charges, but after being enlightened, that in doing so may open up an investigation as to whether or not she provoked him, she decided that it was best not to follow through with it.

Chapter XIV

Fifteen Years down the Road

A thirty-four-year-old Justin Howard, formerly known as prisoner #24601, stood in front of the Bucksdale police department, questioning whether or not he should proceed inside. After five minutes of arguing with himself, he eventually came to the conclusion that he should just go on in. After all, what did he have to lose? He was no longer a prisoner of the State of Mississippi, he had committed no crime. He was just a citizen in search of another person.

As he approached the front desk, he asked a young female officer, "Excuse me ma'am—I mean officer, but you wouldn't happen to know if a Detective Lewis still works here, would ya?" The young officer stopped what she was doing, tapped her pen to her the corners of her mouth, all the while her eyes stayed locked on the ceiling as she contemplated the man's request. "Hmm, do you mean Captain Lewis?" Surprised at her answer, he replied, "Jasper Lewis?" a smile crossed the young officer's face and she confirmed, "Yea, Captain Lewis." A sigh of relief escaped the man, "He wouldn't happen to be in today, would he?"

"He most certainly is, would like me to see if he's available?"

"Yes please."

"And who should I tell him, is asking?"

"#246—Howard—Justin Howard," The young officer gave a rather confused look, then while holding a finger up with one hand and picking a telephone up, in the other. She made a phone call, "Yes sir, this is Officer Pascal, I have a Mr. Justin Howard, who would like to schedule a meeting with you... yes sir, I'll send him right on in."

She shot the man a look of surprise and impression, and said, "He says he's free now, just walk right on back to that hallway just keep following it, till you get to the last office on the left; he'll be waiting for you when you get there. He sounded very delighted that you were here." A brief smile crossed Justin's face, and he made his way down the hall. Justin was surprised to not only see Captain Jasper Lewis, but he also saw Lieutenant

Traci Harmon, alongside with him. The two former Detectives invited Justin into the Captain's office, both of them excited and curious, to hear what all Justin had in store for them.

Lieutenant Harmon closed the door behind them and as they all became seated and made comfortable, Captain Lewis was the first to start, "Justin, how ya been holding up buddy, how's the past fifteen years been treating ya?" Nervously rubbing the arms to the chair that he was sitting in, he replied, "Eh, all things considering I suppose, not too bad. If ya'll don't mind, I'd like to kinda just start things off by saying, that I really appreciate you putting in a good word, to the warden, for me. I wasn't there but about a month before they made me a trustee and had me working back in the kitchen.

And for thirteen years that's where I worked, didn't really get any problems out of anybody, mainly because I never made any problems for other prisoners. I just kept quiet mostly, and managed to hang out with all the old-timers. Oh also, on Sundays I usually helped lead prayer in church. Not too many folks can say they found Christ in prison, but I can honestly say, I might not have ever truly found him if I hadn't gone. Oh but lastly I mostly just wanted to say thanks for believing, that I never killed Mr. Clarke."

Leaning back into his office chair with his hands stretched above his head, Lewis said, "Son, anybody that's ever been gaga for someone else, could've seen how that bitch had you wrapped around her finger so tightly that she could have talked you into doing just about anything. I just hate that things didn't pan out differently; the entire time the trial went on, I prayed that you would get some sense about ya, and blurt out that you didn't do it. Lord knows if you had, we could have built a very strong case against her, and put her away for a long time, maybe even life…because I still don't think she is completely innocent in the death of Dennis Henderson."

"I almost did."

"Why didn't you?" Harmon asked.

"Ma'am, most people think I was clueless about the whole situation, up until the point I punched her in the face. Truth is I started to get an idea, when she first brought up killing some body. However, I just kept telling myself, that she was just overly excited, and that it was all talk and no bite.

"Eventually, I got tired of her talking about killing him and I told her I didn't want to do it anymore; she swore to me that she wouldn't kill him, and that she and I would make a life with each other some other way. She suggested that we have Mr. Clarke over for lunch, so that we could break the news to him, that after we were done with the house, that I would no longer be working for him.

"After we got through eating, the two of them went upstairs, and I stayed in the kitchen, cleaning up; next thing I hear is a thunderous racket rolling down the stairs and I knew right then, she'd killed him. If she hadn't said what she said to me, I might have killed her that very afternoon. But, she put on this act, that she was sorry for what she had done—who she had taken away… she said she was gonna go into the kitchen to get her phone, so that she could turn herself in. The first moments after she left, is probably the most confused I've ever been in my life. I was saddened by the loss of Mr. Clarke, but at the same time, I knew that if Ella was gonna turn herself in; that I would truly be left with nothing.

"At least with her being alive, I still had the false hope that, one day we could be together. Not to mention when we were discussing what would happen in sentencing she said something like: 'You'll only serve five or six years.' And that after I got out, we would make our life together.' I was nineteen and in love and I figured to myself, 'You'll only be twenty-four, it's totally worth it.'"

Harmon leaned over and rubbed Justin on the back. He continued, "At the trial when they sentenced me, and Ella failed to keep eye contact with me, I knew that it was most likely going to be over between us. Then she came and visited me in jail, to break up with me. Even then I didn't really want anything bad to happen to her, I can definitely understand a girl not wanting to be alone for fifteen years.

"Anyway, it wasn't till she told me, that she was happy that I was in prison, and that she hoped bad things would happen to me, and that if the *said* bad things did happen, she would *laugh* at my misfortune. That was when I snapped, that's when I popped that bitch in the nose. If the guards hadn't gotten to me, I probably would have laid into her even more. I guess I figured if I made her ugly, she couldn't do to others, what she had done to me."

"You definitely did a number on her nose." Lewis Remarked, "I'm not certain, but I heard she had to have three or four surgeries done to it. Either way you left a permanent mark on her, I also heard, that it never actually set back straight, and that it's permanently crooked." Justin nodded and said, "Yea, but with that body, and that smile, on top of her royal blue eyes; not to mention all the different mind games that she knows how to play—a fella can look past a crooked nose."

Harmon decided to cut in, "So what are you doing with your life now? You been out for two years, and hadn't gotten yourself rearrested yet, you must be doing something? I gotta say my biggest fear was that you would get institutionalized up there, and become an inmate for life."

"Well, serving time in a kitchen for thirteen years, a man can really only walk away with one skill set; and that's cooking. The only decent thing Ellanece ever did for me was to pay me for painting her house. She left me a savings account with twenty-five G's in it. By the time I walked out of prison, between what she had left for me, and what I had accumulated as a prisoner, I had twenty-eight thousand dollars to my name, seven thousand dollars short of what Ellanece had quoted me last time she visited me.

"At first I thought that I would get work at like a bar and grill, or something similar. But after spending the past thirteen years of my life taking orders, and being treated like a piece of state property, I decided that it was time that I be my own boss and only take orders from me. Via the local classifieds, I managed to find this guy who was selling his old food truck for twelve thousand dollars.

"The Lord did me real good there; man was originally asking for fifteen, but I told him about my situation, so he came down a little for me. Not to mention the truck was already a little bit of a fixer upper anyways. After repairs, buying new equipment, designing a menu, and filing for proper vendor's licenses, I had about thirteen thousand dollars left."

"Where're ya living now?" Harmon asked.

"That's where I decided to be a little bit of cheapskate. Not wanting to spend the rest of my money on lodging, I decided I already had a vehicle that served as transportation and work; so I decided to make it a trifecta, and at night after I close down shop, I roll out a sleeping bag and foam matt, and sleep on the floor."

Shocked at his living arrangements, Jasper couldn't help but ask, "Geez buddy, business that slow?" shaking his head no, Justin replied, "Nah, not really. It's booming actually. Especially on the weekends during game season; I travel between Oxford and Starkville, just depends on who has the bigger game that weekend. I set up shop around the Stadium and just rake in the business."

Lewis and Harmon were both a little dumbfounded as to why a guy with such a successful business; who had spent thirteen years of his life in prison, for a crime that he hadn't committed, was living his life so frugally. Lewis asked, "I don't mean to pry, but what exactly is it that you're saving up for, to live your life in such parsimony?" the room went quiet; Justin contemplated for a moment on whether or not he should say. Lewis chimed in, "Well?"

"300 East Church Street," Justin said in a calm, collected voice, "I noticed it was for sale." Lewis and Harmon exchanged looks. "You sure that's the best idea, I mean if you're looking to settle here in Bucksdale, we welcome you with open arms, but I'm sure you could find some other house to call your home."

Justin shook his head in a grief filled manor, "Nope. That house was the last place, other than a court room, that I stood on this earth as free man, before ya'll took me and Ellanece into questioning. I spent three months of my life, using every technique Mr. Clarke taught me, to paint the innards of that place. And after I buy it maybe one day I'll get around to redoing the outside; them damn illegals, Ellanece hired, to finish that house up, did a sloppy-ass job. I'm surprised Ellanece got what she did for it." Leaning back in his chair, Lewis said, "Well, you'll definitely get that house for a lot less than most its other owners ever paid for it."

"Owners?"

"Oh yea, since Ellanece Mosley sold that joint, it hasn't kept a resident for more than three maybe four years in row."

"Why, what's wrong with it?"

"Foundationally? There ain't a thing wrong that place. The problem people keep having with it, is that Ellanece dropped two damn corpses in that place. However, if you ask people, they'll say she killed one in self-defense, and that you killed the other, out of an uncontrollable rage."

Justin sat nodding his head, with a woebegone look upon his face, and said, "Guess just 'bout everyone in this town thinks that about me." Lewis's eyes squinted, as he threw his arms up to shrug, and said, "Eh—I'd say fifty/fifty. The one's that think ya did are busybodies anyhow, and the ones that don't think ya did, don't care, because it happened so damn long ago.

"But back to my point; people hear about the deaths from the realtors, and they wave a hand at it, thinking: It won't be a problem for 'em. But it never fails, sooner or later, they start getting the notions that the damn place is haunted or something." Justin ran his fingers through his hair, shifting positions in his seat and asked, "Well, is it?" Lewis Chuckled and said, "Gosh no, see what happens is: People hear about that house's history, don't think nothing of it, then once they start hearing weird noises late at night; they forget all about how old the building is, and all they can remember, is how two men died untimely deaths."

"—Violent untimely deaths, at that." Harmon added.

"I can see that. I remember the first couple of nights I spent in that house, after me and Ella would get through with, well ya know—*fooling around*, sometimes you could hear creakin' in the floorboards; like someone was tiptoeing around." Harmon cocked her head to the side and playfully asked, "You don't believe that place is haunted, do you?" Shaking his head, no, he replied, "Nah, I been in that house late at night, I know what old houses sound like."

Lewis cleared his throat and asked, "I hate that I keep digging, and if my questions become too personal, let me know, and I'll stop. I'm merely curious; do you actually have the money for that place? Even though it has been priced far lower than what it went for fifteen years ago, eighty thousand is still a pretty big number." Justin let out a sigh and replied, "Only if you promise that this will be your last personal question."

Lewis nodded, and Justin continued, "I have half of it; I also happen to have an uncle, whom though he may not have the money on hand, he does have the credit to obtain it. And has offered to let me borrow it; on the terms that I pay him back of course. We will purchase the house together, and when I pay him back, in full, he will sign over his half of the house."

Lewis replied, "Good for you, I'm glad to hear that after all that mess you had to go through, that your life is finally starting to piece together. And I just want you to know, that as the Captain of the BPD, the town of Bucksdale welcomes you, whole heartedly." Lewis stood up with his hand out, and Justin did the same, and the two shook hands. Harmon stood up as well, and after the handshake, gave Justin a friendly hug.

As it appeared that the meeting was coming to an end, Justin hesitantly asked, "I must admit, though it's been great catching up with y'all; I have to be honest and say that I also came here with ulterior motives; I was wondering if it might be at all possible for y'all to help me locate Ellanece?" Harmon gasped, out of sheer surprise, bringing her hands up to cover her mouth. Lewis, maintaining his composure, immediately responded, "No, absolutely not!"

"Why not?" Justin implored, hoping he could change their minds, "It's not like I'm asking for y'all to help me make contact with her, I just want to know, at the very least, what city and state she's living in." Standing with his arms crossed, Jasper Lewis spoke out in a very authoritative manner, "Justin Howard, I don't think that you have to hear it from me, to know that woman is responsible for ruining thirteen years of your life. Now, I don't know about you, but if someone were to take away thirteen years of my life; once I was free again, there's only a handful of things that I would want to do to that person; ain't none of them things pretty, and all of 'em is illegal."

"Look, I just want to know which area of the country I ought to steer clear of." Failing to craft a lie, as masterfully as Ellanece could, Lewis could see what Justin was trying to do, so he replied, "I think you'll steer clear of her just fine as long as you stay here in Mississippi."

"After all," Harmon added, "you are about to purchase a home here. Any trips you make outside the state; just keep them sweet and short, and I think you'll do just fine."

"My thoughts, exactly!" added Lewis, "Look man, there is only one way that you and

Ellanece interacting with one another again ends; and that's in tragedy!" Justin shrugged helplessly, "Yea but—you can't blame a guy for wanting revenge."

"You're right, I can't. However, I can stop a good man from making another bad decision, and buddy I promise ya, you go off in search of vengeance, and that woman's either gonna kill you out right. Or you'll be successful in getting the drop you want on her, and you'll go to jail for the rest of your life, for the murder of Ellanece Mosley."

"But what if I could kill her and get away with it?" Justin asked. "I'm sorry pal, neither of us can have this conversation with you. That being said, I've got some things that I have to attend to. Best of luck in getting that Victorian. And please, Justin, you've gotten what most men charged with killing a man, don't get; and that's a second chance—don't go screwin' this one up too." Lewis gave a hearty slap on the back to Justin and exited, Harmon was right behind him, telling Justin to take care of himself as she exited the room, helping escort Justin out of the office.

As they reached the main desk, Harmon stopped Justin before he left and offered him some words of advice, "Hey look man, after you get that home, why don't you focus on settling down and starting yourself a family. I mean, you're still young, and there are plenty of good looking single women in this town."

Justin smiled, blushing just a little bit, and said, "Yea, I 'spose you're right, and I appreciate all that you and Captain Lewis have ever done for me,

I really do. Guess I'll be seeing y'all around." As Justin made his way for the exit, Harmon called out to him one last thing, "Hey Howard, Lewis and I are expecting a house warming party, after you make the buy, so we better be on your guest list." Turning around just before he hit the door, he yelled back, "Count on it!"

Chapter XV

An Invitation

It had been fifteen years since Ellanece Mosley had last seen Justin, the blow to the nose that she had sustained from her taunting, had in fact left her with a permanently crooked nose. Ellanece had relocated to Destine Florida, where a few years back she had wound up meeting and marrying a captain of a charter fishing boat. The man was Captain Nathan Reynolds, and was the third husband, in an already rampantly failing marriage.

This was of coarse all by design. Much like Ellanece's two former husbands, Cpt. Reynolds, had failed to sign a prenuptial agreement, before getting married. Also, he hadn't learned of Ellanece's prior failed marriages, till after their vows had been exchanged.

Long gone were the days of house flipping and being a realtor, with a dash of murder added to the mix. Nowadays Ellanece was all about grifting rich successful men, out of their hard earned wealth. Her MO followed like so: Find a successful, wealthy, entrepreneur. Marry him, make the marriage last three or more years.

Then, she would set the husband up for marital failure, by hiring a beautifully beguiling young woman, who was half her age, to seduce the husband into cheating on her. Then, acting as her own PI, Ellanece would take multiple photographs of the husband in the act of cheating; and after presenting her case and showing the photos of the scandalous husband to her topnotch divorce lawyer, Daryl Lindeman. She would then file for divorce, where she would ultimately wind up taking the poor bastard, for all he was worth. This scheme had worked twice before, and soon she would be lining it up to work for her again.

Meanwhile, back in Bucksdale, Justin was using every moment of his spare time to try and hunt down the elusive, Ellanece Mosley. He had found traces of her in around Birmingham, Alabama and a few showings of her around South Carolina, where she had been using the alias, Stella Mosby. But other than that, he was drawing a bunch of blanks. One night after returning home to 300 East Church Street, from a hard day of working in the food truck, he sat at his computer, with a cold 211 Steel Reserve beer in his hand, once again finding every search attempt that he tried, being utterly useless.

Throp, throp, throp. Justin heard coming from the front door. He got up from where he was seated and went to see who could possibly be banging on his door at eight o'clock at night. He cracked the door open, and much to his surprise he saw Captain Lewis, standing before him. Justin was quick to open the door the rest of the way and with a delighted smile he asked, "Well hey there Cap, what in the world brings you to my door at this hour?"

"Is it alright if I come in?" Lewis asked with an expressionless face. "Sure, of course; is there anything I could offer you to drink? Beer, tea, tap water? It's 'bout all I got I'm 'fraid." Lewis raised an eyebrow and said, "A cold glass of sweet tea sounds like it would hit the spot."

"Of course, hold right there and I'll be right back." Justin made his way back to the kitchen, and when her returned, he was slightly curious when he saw the Captain holding a piece of paper in his hands, a piece which he hadn't been holding, before he went to fetch the glass of tea. As he approached Lewis, he stuck out his hand, which was holding the tea and said, "Here ya go Cap, coldest glass of tea you'll ever find in Bucksdale."

Justin let out an awkward chuckle, and added, "*Naw* I'm just jankin' ya, I don't know if I got the coldest glass or not, I just know it's cold." Lewis took a sip from the glass and as the icy sweet liquid ran down the back of his throat, he smacked his lips a couple of times and said, "Now *that's* a good glass of tea right there, I don't care if it is the coldest or not. You brew this tea yourself, or did ya buy it from the store?"

"No, no, I brewed it 100% all by myself, it's the same tea that I serve on my food truck." Lewis took another sip once again savoring every last sweet drop. "So ugh, what ya got in your hand there, Cap, hope it ain't a warrant?" Justin said lightly with a smile. Lewis looked to Justin as he took yet another sip, and as he finished, he said, "Well now that you mention it—" Justin's face dropped as a warm knot formed in his throat and a chill ran down his spine.

A smile then broke upon Lewis's face and as he playfully slapped Justin on the arm with the paper he continued, "I'm just messin' with ya, bud, I ain't got a warrant. As a matter of fact, the piece of paper that I am currently holding has absolutely nothing to do with you, and is none of your business. That being said, I'm gonna lay it down right here on this table, and when I walk out that door tonight, it's going to stay right here on this table, in your possession." Lewis paused for a moment and slowly placed the folded piece of paper down on the desk.

"Well, if it don't concern me, why you gonna leave it with me?" Lewis cleared his throat and answered, "Listen up, Justin, this is how all this is going to work: Once I leave out that door, I am going to forget that this night ever happened; and that you have any of the information that lies on that sheet.

"Also, whatever it is you decide to do with that information, you do it on your own, or have someone else, other than law enforcement help you do with whatever it is you plan on doing. Lastly, if you decide to do absolutely nothing with the information that comes on that sheet, then that's perfectly fine by me; and don't forget, if you do decide to act on that information and you find yourself caught or in trouble; just remember to leave my name out of it, and I truly do apologize that things didn't work out." Lewis gave a stern nod to Justin, then continued to chug what was left in his glass.

He shook his head setting the glass down, "Man I tell you what, next time I find myself at an Ole Miss game, I'm gonna look for your truck, so that I can get me another glass of that tea. Justin, you have yourself a *good night* and I do hope the best of luck to ya."

The two men shook hands and Jasper Lewis turned around, and exited the humble abode, of 300 East Church Street. Justin waited till Lewis had gotten into his car and drove away, after he saw his cruiser, round the corner, he eagerly grabbed the paper that the Captain had left him; and as he skimmed over the text on the sheet, by the time he finished reading he knew not only the exact location of where Ellanece Mosley resided, but also, a complete list of everywhere she had resided in the past fifteen years. The list also contained the name of the man that she was currently married to, along with the two other ex-husbands' that she had married. Justin now had all that he needed, in order to get his revenge.

A key is placed into a P.O. Box, once turned the door is opened, a hand reached in and pulled out the all that was inside. After closing and locking the door back, the hands begin to flip through all the mail: *Bill, bill, junk mail, magazine, bill—Invitation.* The hands momentarily set aside all of the other envelopes, and focus on the one that is the invite. The hands open it and pull out the document enclosed, and the eyes which belonged to the hands read:

Dear Ellanece M. Reynolds,

     The current owners of 300 East Church Street would be honored for you to attend the 'Historical Marking' of the home on the 18th of October. Seeing as how you were the last person to dramatically restore the home, we the owners feel that it is only right for you to be present at this historic event. We realize that you now reside in Florida, and that you and your husband, probably lead exciting and challenging lives, and we would just like you to know, that we are more than prepared to pay for all travel and lodging expenses, for the both of you.

     We also realize that this home and the town of Bucksdale, may be a very small notch, in a very large list of accomplishments for you; we would just like for you to know how big of a notch your restoration to the home has been, not only to the town, but also, to the people whom reside inside it. Whether you and your husband are or aren't able to attend, please let us know; you can reach us by phone at 601-345-9955 or by e-mail Jim.everett1950@aol.com

Sincerely,
Mr. and Mrs. James Everett

Ellanece couldn't believe what she was reading. Detective Lewis's threat still holding fresh in her mind. She was overwhelmed with several emotions. She was scared because she didn't know if it may be a trap, but if it was sincere, she had this overpowering feeling of pride and honor. She stared at the document for a moment, scrambling her brain, trying to think of how exactly she should process what she had just read.

Her lips scrunched together, and her nose turned up, she walked over to a trash can and held the invitation over it; then in an instance of hesitation, she was now nervously biting her lip, pondering on what was the worst thing that could happen? She brought the letter back in close to her, then skimmed over it once again really fast, and finally settled on the conclusion to sleep on it; so she creased it and slipped it into her purse.

The next morning, she sat alone at the kitchen table, sipping on some coffee, the invitation sitting on the table in front of her. The sound of a talk radio show could be heard in the back ground, meshing with mechanical hum of a ceiling fan above her. Beside the invite, sat her iPhone; she picked her phone up off of the table and dialed the number that was in the letter. She heard three rings before, a person picked up, "Hello," spoke the voice of an elderly gentleman, "this is Jim Everett speaking, may I ask who is calling?"

Ellanece remained silent, she didn't quite know how, or if she should even answer. "*Hello,*" the voice called out once again, "is anybody there?" taking one last sip from her coffee, she gathered her courage and answered, "Hello Mr. Everett, my name is Ellanece Reynolds, I'm contacting you, in regards of the invitation that you and your wife sent me."

"Ah Mrs. Reynolds, I'm so glad to hear from you. My wife and I were a little worried that you might not answer."

"Oh and why's that?" asked Ellanece. Mr. Everett replied, "Well it's no secret that two men lost their lives in this home while you were living here. We would like you to know that nobody in this house, or in this town, blames you or thinks that you are the reason why they died. Everyone is pretty clear, that you were only thrown into situations that were out of your control.

"We also will understand, if the post-traumatic stress of the deaths leaves you not wanting to come back and visit. I just think that it would be a really neat addition, to have the woman responsible for its restoration, present at the ceremony." Ellanece waited for the appropriate time to respond, "Mr. Everett, as much as I would *love* to be present, I must confess that during my stay in Bucksdale, there was a Detective there, by the name of Jasper Lewis, who at the end of the investigation to the murder of Mr. Farrington Clarke, stated that I was *bad* for the town and that I should leave due to the fact that he was banning me, from Bucksdale. So out of respect for his wishes, I'm afraid that I am going to have to decline."

"Oh you're talking about Captain Jasper Louis," Mr. Everett said, "Oh don't you worry about him, he and I are good ole pal's, we've been real close for about the last eight or nine years, all I have to do is tell him the situation, and that it's only for one day or so, and I am more than certain that he'll be okay with it." Still feeling a little nervous about accepting, she answered back with a nervousness in the back of her voice, "I don't remember, how long he told me that I was banned, he seemed pretty adamant about it, so I figured he meant permanently."

"Trust me darling, you'll be fine. I tell you what, if I were to get you a written letter from the Captain, would that get you to come? Remember I'm paying for all of your travel expenses it would almost be like a free vacation—err um, even though you somewhat already live in a perfect vacation spot; you know what I mean."

Feeling confident that Mr. Everett would never get that letter and that he was only talking out of his ass, in order to get her over to Bucksdale, she accepted, "You know what Mr. Everett, you get me a signed doc from the Captain and you have my word that I will be there," not wanting to include her soon to be ex-husband in on any of her former life she added, "oh and one more thing, as far as travel expenses go, it will only be me traveling. My husband has a schedule full of charters that week, so he will not be able to attend."

"Well you have my word Mrs. Reynolds, as soon as we get off the phone, I'm gonna call the

Captain and ask him for that written note of approval, and I trust once you get it, you will come, or is another conformation call in order?" Still confident that she would never see that letter, she said, "Yes sir, Mr. Everett. If I get that letter, I will be there on the 18th, I promise."

Pleased at what he heard he replied, "Splendid, just splendid, well I tell you what, whatever you spend on your way up here I will reimburse you for, in cash, once you arrive; and before you leave we'll figure out how much you need in order to get back home. I hate to cut things short, but I have some other matters that need tending to, we look forward to seeing you next month darling, good buy and do take care." The phone call ended and that was that. The most that she ever expected to hear from Bucksdale again, would be another phone call, from Mr. Everett apologizing for not being able to get the Captain's approval.

A week and a half later, while Ellanece was flipping through her mail, she passed over one envelope with a Bucksdale Mississippi, return address on it. Upon opening it the letter read.

Dear Mrs. Reynolds

As the Captain of Police in Bucksdale, the kind Mr. Everett, whom has purchased the house which you once renovated, has brought it to my attention that you are not the same woman, which I once banned from this town. He has also made me aware of how he would love to invite you to the

home's Historical Marking on the 18th of October,
but that you will not be attending out of respect of
the ban that I put on you, fifteen years ago.
     Mrs. Reynolds that ban was placed on a
very reckless Ellanece Mosley—Mrs. Ellanece
Reynolds however, seems to me to be very
professional with a good reputation to uphold, and I
would love it for Mr. Everett, if you were able to
attend the Historical event, seeing as how I have
lifted any ban, that I ever placed on you.

Sincerely,
Captain of Police, Jasper Lewis

     She couldn't believe what she had just read:
Lewis knows I murdered those two men, she thought
to herself: *why is he just acting as if it never*
happened? She only pondered on it for a moment,
realizing that she had already confirmed that if she
got a note from Lewis, that she would attend the
Historical Marking.
     It didn't even occur to her, that Justin was
out of jail, and that he was free to roam wherever he
pleased, and even if she had, she wouldn't have
thought him to be so ambitious as to start up his
own company, buy him a house; let alone, the house
from which he was framed in. This little trip would
also give Ellanece some time away from her life in
Destin, and a change of scenery would do her well.
Plus, she was also curious to see what all—if
anything—had changed in the Podunk town of
Bucksdale.

Chapter XVI

Karma's Bitch

By the time Ellanece reached Clarke County, it was dusk, almost dark. Ellanece wasn't the type of person to get chills or tingles down her spine, she had done far too many nefarious acts in her life, for her to be that type of person. However, as she passed the sign that read, *Welcome to Bucksdale, Population 2,295* on it, she couldn't help but feel tingles trickling their way down from the top of her spine, all the way down to her tailbone, accompanied with a bad case of horripilation running up and down her arms.

As Ellanece turned her black BMW down the driveway at 300 East Church Street, she found herself slightly vivificated by the sight of the old house. She placed the car into park, then continued to turn the car off; as she stepped out of her car, she even managed to shock herself, by unconsciously snapping a photograph, with her iPhone, as she heard the towns Church Bells, chiming in the distance. She then gave the house a good once over, and was surprised to see that the home was not the way she had left it, (Something she had not expected.) She slowly approached the house very slowly.

As she got within touching distance, she slid her hand across the old wood paneling of the house and could instantly tell that it was not the outer paint job that she had left it with. She continued her way around the house, approaching the front, she stood at the front steps, and as she placed her foot on the first one, she was overwhelmed with a sort of sentimental conviction towards the place, which she hadn't anticipated, on feeling for a place where she had spent such a modicum amount of time at.

After trying her best to dismiss the unexpected feelings, she made it the rest of the way up the steps, and knocked on the door. She could hear the shuffling around, from someone inside and was a little anxious, to see what Mr. Everett looked like. As the brass doorknob turned and the door opened, a humble, fragile looking old man, appeared in front of her, and with a charming smile on his face, he said, "Ah, you must be Mrs. Reynolds."

Ellanece stuck her keys into her purse, only so she could offer a free hand, as his soft old hands met hers, she charismatically replied, "Yes sir, that's me, guilty as charged; and you must be Mr. James Everett" Mr. Everett shook her hand, then kindly stepped out of the way, welcomingly motioning for her to come inside, "By all means ma'am, please do come in."

As she stepped inside of the old home, Ellanece was very taken by the furnishings of the place. Back when she had lived there, it had mostly been furnished with makeshift furniture. The home was full of antique furniture, old paintings and murals; the paint on the walls, the same paint that Justin had put on there, fifteen years ago. It was a detail that she managed to make a mental note of. "I notice you still have the same paint on the walls that was done when I sold the place; what happened with the outside?" With a confused look on his face, Mr. Everett asked, "What do you mean: *What happened to the outside?*"

"I mean…I noticed that the place has a slightly different paint job than the one it had had, when I sold it." The old man shrugged his shoulders and replied, "There have been quite a few owners between you and me. So I suppose one of them must have given the old place a different painting. After all, fifteen years is a long span of weathering, for any building to go through."

Ellanece shrugged the matter off and said, "It's no big matter, truth be told the outer painting was done by a different painter than the one whom did the interior, as you may know, he murdered his boss and was arrested for it. It forced me to have to sell this place quick, if I was gonna make a decent profit on it, so I hired a bunch of wetbacks to do it. They did it quick and the end result—*showed*."

Everett folded his hands together, and said, "Well then, I suppose it all just worked out for everyone." Gesturing with his hands, he continued, "Please, do feel free to walk about the place, I've prepared a guest-bedroom for you upstairs, when you walk up there it will be the room just to your right."

Ellanece thought of asking the old man for help with her luggage, but after a second thought, she decided that he looked much to tenuous, to lug anything, including himself, up that flight of stairs, and the last thing she wanted, was for another body to die in that house, on behalf of her account. "Great," she said cheerfully, "well, I tell ya what I'm going to do: I'm going to go back out to my car, grab my luggage, haul it up yonder, get myself situated, then I'll roam the rest of the place till dinner time—or do I need to get my own dinner? Either one suits me just fine."

Everett waved his hands in the air saying, "No ma'am the Mrs. is out as we speak getting some take out from a place in Stonewall called *Christy's* they have the best food, I swuny to goodness. Think ya might need me to help you, with your luggage?"

Ellanece saw the relieved look on his face, when she told him that there was no need for his assistance, and continued out to her car, to gather her things. Once back inside, just as she got to the landing, she could still vividly see the corpse of Farrington Clarke.

Pausing for a moment, she looked down at the spot where he had died, she thought of the spot in the kitchen where she had killed Dennis, and she was more than certain that if she went to where she had delivered the cleaver to his skull that she would be able to vividly see him, also.

She could never remember what any of her victims looked like, unless she was at the exact location where she had killed them. She shook it off and made it up the stairs with no trouble at all. She made it into her room, which was across the hall from the master bedroom, (her old room) and was pleasantly surprised, to see how quaint, the place had been prepared.

She felt a text alarm buzzing in her back pocket, and so she grabbed it to see who it was from, it was only her husband: *Hey sweets, just checking to see if you made it alright? You said you would text once you arrived?* She quickly replied: *Yea babe, I made it, just got caught up in all the nostalgia of it all. I'll text U N the morning. Luv U, g'night.*

After responding, she realized that she had only twenty percent of battery left, so she began to dig through her bag, in search of her charger: *Where the fuck did I pack that damn charger?* She thought to herself. She dug and dug, searched every pocket and every corner of her suitcase till it finally dawned on her that she had forgotten to pack it: *Guess I'll just zip down to the seven-eleven really quick, and pray that they have one, even if it has to be a shitty little knock of brand.*

Ellanece scurried down the stairs, fumbling to get the keys out of her purse and called out, "Mr. Everett," the voice was faint, but she was able to make out what he said, "In the kitchen darling," She made her way to the kitchen, where Mr. Everett sat at the kitchen table reading a newspaper, "It appears I've gone and done left my phone charger at the danged house, I'm just gonna zip on down the road, to the first gas station I see and *pray* that they have one, that fits my phone. If Mrs. Everett gets home before I get back, don't bother waiting for me, just go ahead and start." Mr. Everett gave a nod as he continued to read his paper, and said, "Nonsense darling, we fully embrace southern hospitality in this house; we'll all eat together, once everyone is in for the night."

As she drove down the road, to the nearest service station, even though it was dark, she could tell that little to nothing had changed in the town. She was amazed to see businesses, like Skidmore's Restaurant, still open for business. She pulled into the seven-eleven, and as she entered, she had forgotten how eerie small town gas stations could be at night.

Entering through the front sliding doors, she noticed that the store was desolate. The only other person in the store, being the clerk, an obese black woman, who seemed to mean-mug her, every time she looked up from her phone, to make sure that she wasn't stealing anything.

She found a cheap knock off charger for around fifteen dollars, purchased it, then hastily made her way back to her vehicle and continued to make her way back to 300 East Church Street. As she drove down the road, she had rolled the window down, and felt the lukewarm Mississippi night's air, which was rather common for an October's night, down south.

Being overwhelmed with relief as she pulled into the driveway of 300 East Church Street, that there weren't any new vehicles there; she figured Mrs. Everett must not have returned. However, it was now fully dark, and Ellanece could hardly see any lights on in the house, mainly just the one light from her bedroom: *Old-timers,* she thought to

herself: *always rummaging around in the fuckin'*
dark.

She tried to make her way in through the
back door, like she used to do, back when she had
lived there, but the door was locked, she could
make out a little bit of light coming from kitchen,
she tapped on the window, hoping Mr. Everett
would hear her. But after a few moments of waiting,
she decided she would just make the trek around the
house, and enter through the front.

She made her way in through the front door
and as she stood in the foyer of the home, she was
relieved that it had been left illuminated. She made
it a point to place her newly purchased charger into
her purse, and continued her way into the living
room, which was almost completely blacked out,
only being lit from the streetlights out side, she
could see from the door frame into the kitchen,
where it looked as if it was only being lit, by the
overhead stove light. "Mr. Everett," she called out,
"I'm back, so when I enter the kitchen don't be
startled, okay."

It was almost a straight shot from the foyer
doorframe, through the living room, to the kitchen's
doorframe. Gracefully whisking herself though the
darkness, into the kitchen, she could see the
silhouette of Mr. Everett sitting at the end of the
table in the dark. She figured he might have just
dozed off, sitting in the darkness like that, so
Ellanece started sliding her hand around the wall to
try and find a light switch, so that she could wake
him up.

She kept sliding her hand around blindly,

her rings scratching across the painted walls, hoping that at any moment she wound find the switch: *Oh just where the hell—wha-ha!* She flipped the light on, and as she triumphantly thought: *found it!*

She heard a voice that didn't belong herself, or to Mr. Everett, a voice she hadn't heard in fifteen years, "Long time no see, sweet heart," The very sight of Justin almost made her faint. Composing herself as best she could, as she hugged her purse with one hand, and clung to the counter to hold herself up with the other, "Justin, uh, um… you—"

"—Save it bitch," he interrupted. Ellanece quickly thought about running back towards the front door, "Don't even think about it," he said, "By now I'm sure *Mr. Everett* has the front door dead bolted by now, just as all the other entrances/exits have been dead bolted, and the only two people who have the keys to these locks would be me and *Mr. Everett*, whom has locked the front door from the outside, so that I don't have to worry about you hunting him down, and killing him for the key." Ellanece had calmly placed a hand into her purse and she responded, "Well just so you know, I ain't in the business of killin' no more." Shaking his head Justin replied, "I'll be damned, it's like a fucking switch; you just casually turn on and off, don't you?"

"I ain't quite sure what you're talkin' about?"

"The *good ole girl* act, I know that's not how you really talk, so I suggest you cut it out!" Justin got up from where he was seated, and took a few steps towards her, and that's when Ellanece placed a hand on her black and pink .380 Taurus pistol and whipped it out of her purse and yelled, "Hold it right there!" Justin shrugged his shoulders and with an insouciant chuckle he said, "What? You really think that you are going to shoot me, in *my* own house and simply get away with it? Nah—and FYI, I'm unarmed so it's gonna look really fuckin' bad for you, if you do in fact decide to shoot me." Ellanece confusedly asked, "Hold up, I thought that this was—"

"—*Mr. Everett's* house? No sweetie, I'm afraid not. You see, this is *my* house, that *I* own, and *Mr. Everett,* is in actuality, George Woodberry, Dennis Henderson's uncle. Now why don't you just put the little pea-shooter away, and have yourself a seat. Hell, I'll even grab ya beer, if ya want one; you know, *for old time's sake*." Ellanece slowly crossed to the table, while saying, "I'll take a seat, but the gun stays out."

"And the beer?"

"Sure, I'll take one." Justin crossed to the fridge, all the while keeping an eye on Ellanece, opened the door, brought out two beers. Placed one on the table and slid it to Ellanece. She placed her gun and purse down, only long enough to open her beer, then quickly picked it back up.

She then eyeballed her purse, placed the beer down, and with her free hand, dug inside of her purse till she produced a prescription bottle of Adderall, and flawlessly opened it with the single hand, and shook two pills into her mouth, replacing the top to the bottle, she tossed it back into her purse, and then grabbed the beer, and took a swig to down the pills. Justin cracked the top to his beer, and added, "Jesus, you're still popping those damn things?" Ellanece rolled her eyes, then shook her pistol at him, in a gesture that hinted for him to stop talking.

"Oh yea, and Ella, baby, don't forget that Captain Lewis knows you are here in town, can't go forgetting that nice forgiveness letter he wrote ya, welcoming you back into the town. So if you do wind up killing me, just keep it in the back of your mind that he will know beyond the shadow of a doubt, that *you* killed me, and he will also know, that you are a serial killer, and that means that the FBI gets involved. Have fun explaining to your husband, Captain Nate, why you gotta get out of dodge. Not to mention once he finds out who you really are, and what all you've really done in your past; you really think that he is going to want to stick it out with you? My bet is that he runs for the fuckin' hills."

Ellanece's lips tightened and she said in miffed tone, "So just why exactly, have you brought me back here?" Justin pulled a chair up beside her and as he sat down, "If it's dying that you're scared of, worry not. I ain't gonna kill you." Justin stroked her cheek with the back of his hand, "After all Ella, you're my first—*everything*! I can't kill the woman who took me upstairs in that bedroom up there, and made a real man out of me." Ellanece took a sip of her beer and shrugged, "Then why? You want to try and get one more *lay* out of me? If that's the case, then come on baby I'll jump your bones, right here on this here table."

Justin shook his head, "All I want is an honest to God confession, I want to know how many you've killed, and I want to know why you felt you had to go and kill 'em." Ellanece was completely bewildered, "That's it?" she chuckled, tossing the gun down onto the table and taking another sip of her beer. Justin asked, "How many?"

Ellanece shrugged her shoulders placing her beer down, "I don't know, more than fifteen, less than twenty." Shaking his head, he replied, "You mean to tell me that you can't even remember the exact number? Geez lady, tell me you at least remember all of their names?" She shrugged once again, with a shitty little smile on her face, "Half of 'em at best, honestly I never would have been able to tell you the Henderson kid's name, if you hadn't brought it up."

"Has *sex* been involved every time?"

"Of course it has! With the exception of Farrington's case; I had no interest in fucking him, only you, and in every sense of the word." Justin got up from his seat and shouted, "Why?" Ellanece got up from her chair and placed a hand on Justin's chest in a very seductive manner, "Because babe, *sex and murder* are the two most thrilling things that one can ever participate in, why not let them intertwine for the *ultimate experience*."

She ended her sentence in a crisp hiss, and slid her hand down from his chest, and worked it into his pants, while passionately engaging him in a kiss, ending the kiss by biting his lower lip, as she wrapped her fingers around his privates, Justin whispered, "Take my shirt off," Doing as she was told, she pulled his shirt off, and as she gazed upon his chest, she saw a tiny microphone, taped to his chest, with the wire rung over his shoulder and down his back into his back pocket.

Ellanece jerked away violently, as Justin stated, "That's right bitch—I've recorded every word you just said. You know, for someone who has spent their entire life grifting and playing people, you'd think that you would know when you were being played."

Her face was red out of anger; she let out a yell, and stood up so fast, that the table slid back, instinctively she had kept a grip on her pistol, and as she wrapped her finger around the trigger, she raised her arm to aim and shoot, that's when two uniformed Officers came out from the darkness of the living room, shouting, "Put the gun down!"

Chapter XVII

Catching a Killer

Two months prior to the events occurring in the last chapter*:*

Throp, throp, throp an old man heard, rapping at his front door, the man was a bit slow getting out of his old rocker, and as he was half way to the door, he heard a second wave of throping: *Throp, Throp,* "—Hold on, just a minute, I'm on my way," the old man yelled out. Cracking the door open, he asked, "May I help you?" The man on the other side of the door replied, "Yes sir, or at least I hope you can; are you Mr. George Woodberry?" the old man tilted his head with a sigh and said, "I am,"

"My name is Justin Howard; I live a few towns over in Bucksdale,"

"I'm familiar with the town," the old man replied with a grimace.

"Yes sir, you see I live at 300 East Chur—" Woodberry tried to slam the door in Justin's face, but Justin slid his boot in the door to jam it. "—Mr. Woodberry please hear me out," trying his best to shut Justin out, he replied, "I ain't answering no more questions! That boy's been dead for fifteen years, and I don't care what any of you *fuckers* say, he didn't try to rape nobody; ya already worried his damn mother into the grave, with all your questions, and you're not about to get me too!" Doing his best to wiggle his face into what little opening was left, in between the door and its frame, Justin called out, "I know! I can clear Dennis's name!"

Justin felt the pressure of the door remove from his face, and Mr. Woodberry asked with moderate question in his eyes, "Ain't nobody tried to clear him in the past; who the hell are you to all of a sudden be concerned?" catching his breath and dusting himself off, Justin replied, "My Name is Justin Howard, and fifteen years ago, the same *bitch* that murdered your nephew, framed me, for the murder of my boss."

Mr. Woodberry, scratched his chin for a moment, "Oh yea, rumors had it, that you and the girl, were trying to pull one over on your boss, by making his death look like an accident, but in the interrogation, you cracked, admitting to everything, saying that the girl had nothing to do with it, and that it was all your idea." Shaking his head Justin corrected him, "Well the rumors are half true. Ellanece and I were planning on doing him in, but at the last moment, I changed my mind, she had me going for a minute, that if I didn't want to go through with it, that we wouldn't; but then she wound up killing him anyways. I was gonna tell the cops she did it; but somehow or another, she tricked me into thinking that she was really in-love with me and that she would actually wait for me, to get out of jail." Woodberry nodded his head, "And I'm guessing she never waited, huh?"

"Nope." An awkward silence passed between the two; finally, Woodberry broke it by saying, "Please, have a seat; and tell me your plan on clearing my nephew's name?" Justin took a seat, and began, "Alright, I was sentenced to Jail for fifteen years; I was released early for good behavior. Long story short through being self-employed I have managed to buy back the home, where my life got screwed up, 300 East Church Street."

Woodberry shrugged with a very dumbfounded gaze upon his face and asked, "Why on earth would you want to go and do a thing like that for? The place can't be anything but bad memories?" Justin waved him off, "Eh I guess you could say the memories are bitter sweet, but the real reason why I bought the home, was so that I could lure Ella—Mrs. Reynolds—back to the home, and get a confession out of her."

"I don't know, that plan seems a little too, *out of the movies*, for me. What, are you just going to call her up out of the blue, tell her you bought the house, ask her over for a few drinks, and then wait till she's liquored up enough to get her to spill the beans?" Justin threw his face into the palm of his hand, and shook his head, "No sir, my plan is a little more grounded and elaborate than that. Trust me; this isn't some two-bit plan that I concocted over-night. I've been plotting this whole thing for several years. I promise you, my plan will work."

Woodberry motioned with his hands, to continue on with the plan, "You are going to send her a fake invitation, as one, James Everett, the most recent owner of the home; in the invitation, you are going to inform her, of how the home is getting its own historical marker, and that you would *love* for her to be present for it. Now, I don't have any dates set in stone, just as of yet, but I do have a false e-mail, and phone number." Justin reached into his pocket and pulled out a phone, "Look, this burner-phone that I have, receives both the fake number and e-mail, so you will be able to get into contact with her." Justin tossed the phone to Woodberry, who was still a bit unsure of the plan.

"What all am I supposed to say, if she calls," asked Woodberry, "I don't want to scare her off, and I've really never been all that good at acting." Throwing a palm up in the air, Justin replied, "The way that I plan on writing the invitation, will pretty much have her asking you all the basic questions, and all you gotta do, is reassure her a free trip to Bucksdale, and how important it is that she be here. I'm telling you, curiosity will get the better of her. All I need to know, is if you are on board?" Woodberry thought for a moment, then with a stern nod, threw out his hand saying, "For my late-sister's sake; I accept. All she ever wanted, was to believe that her boy was innocent."

Justin shook Woodberry's hand and added, "And that's exactly what we are about to do. Once we get her over here, we'll wait till she gets good and settled, I'll be hiding in one of the guest bedrooms, with a wire strapped to me. I also plan to have the cops nearby, so that if things go south, they can be ready at any moment's notice.

One week later, Justin returned to Mr. Woodberry's house, with a finished invitation, so that the two could go over it, and all of the possible questions, that he might be able to expect from Ellanece. After an hour or two of tossing ideas back and forth, Woodberry felt that he was ready for the task at hand. Justin mailed the invitation off later that day, and four days later, Mr. Woodberry received the call from Ellanece. After he hung up the phone, the first thing he did was give Justin a ring. "Hello," answered Justin. "Yea kid, it's me. I just got off the phone with Mrs. Reynolds; I got good and bad news." after a slight pause, Justin replied, "Let's hear the bad first,"

"The bad news is that she says, Lewis put a ban on her, fifteen years ago and that she won't set foot back in this town, without his written approval...I may have fudged things up, but went on ahead and told her that I could get a letter from the Captain telling her that she was welcome back to the town. Otherwise, without that letter, she made it pretty clear that she wasn't stepping foot in this town."

Justin shook his head, replying, "That is bad news, Captain Lewis made it pretty clear that I wasn't to get him or the police involved." Woodberry cleared his throat, you could always just, forge a letter? Besides don't forget, you haven't heard the good news."

"Yea, and that is?" Justin asked. George Woodberry couldn't keep the smile off of his face, as he replied, "You were right...I could hear the intrigue in her voice. She is definitely curious."

Later that night Justin pulled up outside of Captain Lewis's house in his food truck, and said a prayer, before exiting the vehicle; it was around eight thirty, and as he began to make his way up Lewis's porch, he hadn't made it up the third step, before the front door flung wide-open, and out stepped Lewis, with a Colt 1911, strapped to his side. "You better have a damn good reason for visiting me at my home, at this time of night." Justin stood with his hands in the air and said, "Look sir, I just need some friendly advice," Lewis sagaciously flicked the top strap of his holster, off of his 1911 and said, "Some friendly advice might tell you to get the hell off my property."

Justin brought his hands from up above his head to out in front of him, clasping his hands together in a prayer-like formation, and pleaded, "Captain Lewis, please, I know how to get her here, I'm pretty sure I know how I can get her to confess, but what I don't know, is what to do afterwards? I need cops to be there, so that I can get the bitch arrested." Lewis refastened the strap over his 1911 and slung his head back, motioning for Justin to join him inside.

Closing the door behind them, so that they could talk in private, Lewis said, "You know kid, when I gave you that docket on Ellanece, I was really hoping that you would just flip through the pages, realize that she was a married woman, and would decide to let bygones be bygones, and move on with the rest of your life."

Justin immediately became animated with vexation and shouted, "I should be the sole owner of C.A.R.P.S right now! I should have a nice big brand new house, with a big brand new truck, along with a beautiful wife and kids. That *cunt* stole all of that from me, including thirteen years of my life. And please, spare me the: *You did it to yourself* run about, I won't rest until somebody, be it myself or someone else, brings Ellanece Mosley to justice."

Lewis let an enervated sigh escape him, "Sounds to me, what you want to do is set up a sting operation," with a new elated look of excitement in his eye, Justin replied, "Are you saying you're gonna help me?"

"Dammit son, I want to see you get the closure that you deserve. If you can get Ellanece here in town, I'll get you set up with a wire, and if you can get a confession out of her, I'll put her behind bars. But keep in mind that in order for the confession to hold up in a court of law, you cannot have harmed or even threatened to harm her in any way, shape, or form."

On the day of Ellanece's arrival, Justin, Captain Lewis, Lt. Harmon, Officer Nolan, Officer Russell, and Mr. Woodberry stood on the front porch of 300 East Church Street. In the early morning hours plotting out how everything was going to play out. Lewis was pacing back and forth as he lectured, "We estimate Mrs. Reynolds arrival time to be somewhere in the mid to late afternoon hours. That means that we are going to be playing a little bit of a waiting game with her,"

Lewis pointed to the two uniformed officers, "you two, don't move in until Mr. Howard has received one or more murder confessions, or unless the situation turns violent. We do suspect Mrs. Reynolds to have at one time been an active serial killer, so having a weapon on her person, is to be expected. Just because she draws the weapon, does not mean that you move in. Violent threats are like currency to people like her, she will use them freely, in order to get what she wants. That being said let's wrap things up; we'll meet back here at two o'clock and assume our positions."

Later on that day, towards three in the afternoon, Justin along with the two uniformed police officers, hid in the upstairs Master bedroom, across the hall, from the room that was set up for Ellanece. As they quietly sat, they could hear the muffled conversation going on between Woodberry and Ellanece. The original plan was to wait till dark and have Woodberry distract her outside while they moved into place, but they were given a lucky window, when Ellanece announced that she had to run down the road, to get something from the gas station.

Hearing her car pull out of the driveway, Lewis's voice came on over the radio, "Where the hell is she going, what's going on, did she get spooked?" one the officers with Justin, Officer Nolan, answered, "No sir, we believe that she is only going down the road to get something, booze, snacks, tampons, we're not really clear but we are certain that she will be returning in a short while."

Lewis quickly started up his vehicle which was parked around the corner, and parked it in front of the house. Leaving the vehicle running, he ran inside and yelled out, "I need everyone in the kitchen now; we don't know how long we have before she returns."

Justin and the two Officers came trampling down the stairs, busting into the kitchen. After everyone was gathered, Lewis handed out orders, "Nolan, Russell—secure all of the exits, except for the front door, do it now," the two Officers did as they were told and exited the kitchen. "I want all of the lights in the house off," said Lewis, "all of them, except for the stove light here in the kitchen, the foyer, and her bedroom upstairs; the sun should have completely set by the time she gets back so we are going to use the night and its shadows to our advantage."

The two officers returned back to the kitchen and confirmed that all of the exits were locked. "Alright," said Lewis, resuming his orders, "Justin, I want you to stay here in the kitchen but sit at the end of the table so that your face will remain hidden. Woodberry, I want you Nolan, and Russell to wait in the darkness of the living room; this is where the big gamble is going to take place, there isn't a light switch on the wall of the living room connected to the foyer, however, the stove light from the kitchen should illuminate a well enough path that she won't try to turn on any lights, till she gets to the kitchen anyway. Its go time guys, let's make this happen." Lewis exited the house, got back into his cruiser and circled back around the block.

Where the last Chapter left off:

Justin whispered, "Raise my shirt," Doing as she was told she pulled his shirt off, and as she gazed upon his chest, she saw a tiny microphone, taped to his chest, with the wire rung over his shoulder and down his back into his back pocket. Ellanece jerked away violently, "That's right bitch, and I've recorded every word you just said. You know for someone who has spent their entire life, grifting and playing people, you'd think that you would know when you were being played."

Ellanece's face was red out of anger; she let out a yell and turned around to the table, picking up her gun, that's when Officers Nolan and Russell came out from the darkness of the living room, shouting, "Put the gun down!" she dropped the gun out of the consternation of the two booming voices, and was apprehended on the spot.

Moments later, you could hear the sound of screeching tires coming to a halt from out front; you could hear the sound of the front door being unlocked, and shortly afterwards, in walked Captain Jasper Lewis, and Lieutenant Traci Harmon. As the uniforms read her, her rights, Ellanece shouted at Lewis, "This is fucking entrapment!" Justin who was finishing putting his shirt back on, got in her face and said, "No, this is *justice!*" Harmon and Lewis synchronously replied, "*Agreed!*"

Ellanece continued, "I want to know what exactly it is that I am being arrested for?" Lewis walked up behind Justin and said, "Firstly: Your being arrested for being in violation of a ban that I placed on you, fifteen years ago, that I believe stated, *you were to never return to this town.*" Ellanece wriggled in her cuffs, "Again, *entrapment,* you sent me a letter, welcoming me back to the town, lifting the ban, cocksucker!"

Lewis shrugged his shoulders and replied with a dumbfounded look on his face, "I don't recall ever writing such a letter?" Justin looked over to Lewis, then back to Ellanece and with a shitty grin on his face, chimed, "Oh yea—that was me again. I almost didn't believe that you would fall for it; I sure am glad I took Mr. Woodberry's advice that you wouldn't know the difference, even if your life depended on it."

Ellanece just rolled her eyes, "Fine, then I'll press forgery charges, you little prick, hope you have fun going back to the Pen!" Lewis placed a hand on Justin's shoulder and said, "Those charges will never stick and you know it, you're just pissed because after all of these years, the gig's finally up, and you finally now have to pay for the all of the murders that you have committed."

She was only silent now, pouting like a child, cheeks red with anger, perspiration lining her brow line. "Lewis chimed in one last time, "Again, don't look so upset Mrs. Reynolds, after all you're only forty-three, you've been married three times, after your husband hears the news you'll probably also be divorced three times, I'd say that up until now, you've led one hell of a life.

"Not too many serial killers can say that about themselves, most can only say that they were sad pathetic introverts, with mommy and daddy issues." Ellanece's only response, "Shit in your damn hand, pig; I want my lawyer!" Lewis just shook his head, and said to Officer Russell, "Get her out of here, and take her down to the station for further questioning." Russell did as he was told, and escorted Ellanece out to a patrol car.

Lewis and Harmon looked over to Justin, Harmon asking the question, "So how's it feel to know that she's going to be locked up, if not for good, then she'll be sentenced to death row." Justin nodded and replied, "Right. For the first time since all this shit happened, fifteen years ago, my life finally feels, *right*." Lewis looked around the room then stated, "It's a shame you can't keep all of this really nice furniture, that you used to stage for *Mr. Everett's home*,"

"Yea," Justin replied, "tomorrow it all goes back to Simmons Furniture Outlet, it sure was nice of them though, to let me furnish my house for as little cost as they did; if Ella had seen my real furniture she would have definitely known something was up."

"What all *does* belong to you?" questioned Harmon. "None of it's here right now; it's all being stored in the Simmons Warehouse. But what would normally be here would be a used sofa in the living room, along with a used recliner, and an old flat screen TV. The bed in my room is actually mine but not the bed in the room that I prepared for Ella. Other than that, the only other things I own really, is a fold out table and chairs that I've been using as a kitchen table." Lewis let out a relaxing sigh, exhaling, "Ah, the bachelor life, so glad I don't have to live it anymore." Harmon nudged Justin on the shoulder, "So what're your plans from here on out? You're a free man, with a brand new, *Ella-free*, life."

"Well," Justin replied, "business is actually really good up around Oxford, so I'm most likely going to sell this place, and move up that way. I'd love to stay here, it's just this place has too many memories, there's not a day that goes by, that I don't see Mr. Clarke's body laying at the foot of those damned stairs. The only reason why I ever even came back to this town, to buy this house, was so I could put Ella in her rightful place, and now that I have, I can finally move on."

Lewis patted Justin on the back, with one hand, then stuck his other hand out to shake his hand, and said, "Well bud, wherever you wind up settling, I hope you find yourself a pretty little lady, and start a pretty little family, you deserve to live a happy life."

"Absolutely," added Harmon, "if anyone deserves a second chance, it's you, pal." Lewis looked at his watch and said, "Well, looks like it's about time that we get out of your hair." Justin nodded and said his good buys to the Captain and Lieutenant, and as he shut the door after they exited, Justin knew that his ordeal was truly over.

Ellanece M. Reynolds, who later changed her last name back to Mosley, after getting divorced from her husband; eventually confessed to committing sixteen different murders, across five southern states. Ellanece Mosley was tried and sentenced to death row, where she would await an execution by lethal injection.

After the final hearing for Ellanece, George Woodberry, visited the grave site of his deceased sister, to tell her the news of how her son died an innocent victim, and that his murderer was found guilty, and given a justified sentencing to death. Justin Howard sold the estate of 300 East Church Street, and moved to a suburban community just outside of Oxford Mississippi, where he set up his own restaurant, and still resides to this day, with his lovely wife and two children.

Author's Note

The town of Bucksdale, Mississippi is loosely based off of a town called Quitman, located in Clarke County Mississippi where there actually resides an address of 300 East Church Street, and at this address sits my late Grandmother Ruth's prized Victorian. The restaurants mentioned are all real as well, and all serve phenomenal food. Since Bucksdale is loosely based on Quitman, I've taken occasional liberties with the geography of the state of Mississippi, and the street map of Bucksdale, only to hasten the advancement of the story.